SARA ORWIG

Books have always opened a magical world for me. As an only child in a house of parents and grandparents, I spent every possible moment reading. In addition, I had a free movie pass that provided me with another fantasy world – stories with dashing, swashbuckling heroes and beautiful heroines. For my sixth birthday, my grandfather built a small wooden desk where my first writing attempts were about Mr. Woo, an adorable yellow cat. I still love to read. My active imagination has always

continued on inside back cover

LOVESWEPT • 58

Sara Orwig
Oregon Brown

"Will you play 'When a Man Loves a Woman,' please?" Charity asked in a breathless whisper.

" 'When a Man Loves a Woman,' " the deejay repeated, putting on the record, then coming back to the phone. "Charity, want to know how I'd love a woman?"

"Yes," she murmured, blushing slightly in the darkened bedroom. She wanted to hear but she didn't want to. She held her breath as he whispered throatily, "I'd hold you next to my heart, darlin'. I'd kiss you all night long, kiss you so slowly, cover every inch of you, your throat, your mouth, your sweet shoulders, with my lips. I want to touch you, Charity . . ."

WHAT ARE *LOVESWEPT* ROMANCES?

They are stories of true romance and touching emotion. We believe those two very important ingredients are constants in our highly sensual and very believable stories in the *LOVESWEPT* line. Our goal is to give you, the reader, stories of consistently high quality that may sometimes make you laugh, sometimes make you cry, but are always fresh and creative and contain many delightful surprises within their pages.

Most romance fans read an enormous number of books. Those they truly love, they keep. Others may be traded with friends and soon forgotten. We hope that each *LOVESWEPT* romance will be a treasure—a "keeper." We will always try to publish

LOVE STORIES YOU'LL NEVER FORGET
BY AUTHORS YOU'LL ALWAYS REMEMBER

The Editors

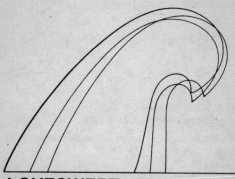

LOVESWEPT · 58

Sara Orwig
Oregon Brown

BANTAM BOOKS
TORONTO · NEW YORK · LONDON · SYDNEY · AUCKLAND

OREGON BROWN

A Bantam Book / August 1984

*LOVESWEPT and the wave device are trademarks of
Bantam Books, Inc.*

ISBN 0-553-21663-5

Published simultaneously in the United States and Canada

---

*Bantam Books are published by Bantam Books, Inc. Its
trademark, consisting of the words "Bantam Books" and
the portrayal of a rooster, is Registered in U.S. Patent and
Trademark Office and in other countries. Marca Registrada.
Bantam Books, Inc., 666 Fifth Avenue, New York, New
York 10103.*

PRINTED IN THE UNITED STATES OF AMERICA

O   0 9 8 7 6 5 4 3 2 1

To Mary Grigg—and with thanks also to Grace Slaughter, George Dawes, and Tim Orwig

One

A bright full moon splashed an alabaster radiance over Enid, Oklahoma, and onto the shingled roof of a red brick, single-story house on Oak Street. Moonbeams skittered over immaculately landscaped beds of pink petunias, purple periwinkles, scarlet roses, and danced on the roof of the patio across the back of the house. Just beyond the shadowy patio, shades were drawn on a south bedroom window. Inside, the faint red glow from a radio dial added orange tint to the old-fashioned maple furniture. In the hushed silence of midnight, a slumberous, baritone voice, husky and full-bodied, whispered, "Darlin', I've missed you. It's been so lonely . . ."

Charity Jane Webster stretched, her head rubbing the pillow, slender arms and legs brushing pale, cool sheets while the deep male voice sent a frothy tickle down her spine. She ran her fingers through the tangle of yellow curls that capped her head, a sigh of yearning escaping her full, curved lips. The radio dial's red glow kissed her wide cheekbones and her thick golden eyelashes.

"Darlin', here's one just for you, an oldie, 'Days of Wine and Roses.' "

She listened to the music, waiting for it to end to hear the velvety masculine voice that would strum over her quivering nerves. She was so lonesome. The late-night hours were the worst time of all. During the day she was busy, too busy to want someone, to really need someone else, but the long, empty nights were torment. She had found on station KKZF a late-night program of mood music called "Nighttime," with a disc jockey who had a golden voice, a rich, resonant baritone that floated into the bedroom, as tangible as a touch, nuzzling her senses, eliminating a fraction of her loneliness. Rory Craig Runyon. Each night she attempted to picture a face to go with that sexy, sensational voice.

He came on again, a lazy, raspy tiger's purr, rumbling up from his chest. "Darlin', did you like that? I hope so. It's one of my favorites. Now, darlin', it's your turn." He said the last in a breathy timbre that spooned hot liquid syrup down her spine and into her bloodstream. Each word in his special voice, like the notes of a cello, brushed a nebulous stroke over her flesh, a caress, making her tingle and ache, yet not feel so empty and alone. "It's your turn. . . ." The words, said in Rory Runyon's voice, held innuendo, implied intimacy.

"Darlin', let me know what you'd like to hear. Come on, give me a call. You know my number. It's eight four three . . ."

Charity blinked in the darkness. Each number

sank into her brain, keyed in permanently. Her hand drifted to the phone, then hesitated. Feeling ridiculous, she frowned at the radio dial. Should she call or not? The only answer was Rory Craig Runyon's thick, torrid voice pulsing slowly into her being. "Come on, darlin'. Let me know what you want to hear."

A phone buzzed on the program. Then Rory Runyon's marvelous voice whispered, "Hi, there." Pause. "Nancy, darlin', I thought you'd never call." Another pause. Charity wished she had called. "Sure. I'll play, 'You Don't Bring Me Flowers,' " he promised in a plaintive, hushed tone. "I'll play it, Nancy, just for you. Hang on there, darlin', and we'll listen together." Music came on and the voice went off.

Next time, she would call in. What harm would there be in a phone call? What harm would there be in calling a DJ and requesting a song? She looked at the door. She shouldn't be lonesome with her great-aunt down the hall, but Aunt Mattie was little company at night. Charity rubbed her forehead. What a muddle life could become! A year ago she had graduated from college with a degree in landscape architecture, had started her own small firm with money from her grandfather's brother, Uncle Hubert, and had been dating Ted Farnsworth. Now her business had failed, she had broken up with Ted months ago, and Uncle Hubert had died. With Uncle Hubert gone, Charity had only two relatives—Uncle Hubert's wife, Aunt Mattie, who was actually a great-aunt by marriage, and her mother's sister, Aunt Ziza. And whatever husband Ziza had at the moment. The mere thought of Ziza made Charity frown. She had lived with Ziza the first year after her parents' death, while Ziza divorced Roger, husband number five, and married Wendell, husband number six. Charity gave a small prayer of thanks she didn't have to take care o Ziza. All she had to worry about were her debts, he employment, and Aunt Mattie. Charity moaned, bu then her glum thoughts were interrupted by Ror Runyon. "Did you like that, Nancy? Good. Call again darlin'. 'Night."

" 'Night." It became two syllables in his soft mid western drawl. *'Nii-aight.* She envisioned sky-blu eyes, curly black hair, a black-haired Tom Selleck Her sigh was audible.

"Here's another goodie for a balmy Sunday night Have you been outside tonight? It's great. Stars lik diamonds on black satin, spread across the heaven as far as you can see. There's a little breeze runnin across the prairie, racing over ripe wheat fields, just soft touch of warm May wind. A night for love, a nigh to hold your hand . . . Let's add a little music to th magic of the evening. Let a spring breeze carry thi song to your heart, darlin'. Straight from me to you.

Charity blinked and swallowed hard. A song bega playing, a haunting melody that relaxed Charity' tense muscles. The melodic voice singing the balla wasn't as enticing as the DJ who put on the record The voice sang, ". . . tied up in red ribbons and blu paper . . ."

She blinked. Paper. She wished she hadn't hear that word. The troubles of the day came rushin back. She had inherited Uncle Hubert's house, th care of Aunt Mattie, his newspaper, *The Enid Times* and a bushel of trouble. She didn't know anythin about running a paper. She could sell it. There was buyer. He lived right behind Uncle Hubert and Aun Mattie's. His yard backed up to theirs, but she hadn met him or looked over the high board fence that sep arated the two yards. Mr. O. O. Brown. It dawned o her suddenly that Mr. Brown was Rory Craig Runyon's boss. O. O. Brown owned the radio station and wanted to own the newspaper. But did she really want to sell? What would she do with the house and Aunt Mattie? What about her debts from her company?

She rolled onto her stomach to stare at the red glow from the radio. The music stopped. The inviting, lulling, sensuous voice came on again. "Now, darlin', it's your turn. Call me, I want to talk to you. Let me know what you like. Do you remember my number. . . ?"

How could she forget? She sat up, covers dropping around her hips as she dialed swiftly, hoping she would get the call through before the line was tied up.

The cottony words came through the telephone receiver into her ear, into her system. Something happened to Charity's heart. It stopped for a breathless minute. Dummy, she chided herself. But she couldn't speak, couldn't breathe. "Hi, Rory, this is . ." She paused. Why hadn't her parents given her a sexy, contemporary woman's name? Something like Raquel or Brooke or Stephanie? She said, "This is Charity." It came out a squeak. She shook her head. What was the matter with her? Loneliness had unhinged her!

"Charity, darlin'."

Never, never in her life, not with Ted or anyone else, had her name been said in such a manner by such a voice. She melted into warm butter that could barely cling to the phone. She sank down in the bed feeling hot, idiotic, ten years younger than twenty-four, and she loved every second of it!

"Did you just catch the program or are you a regular?"

"I'm a regular. I love your program," she said softly in a daze. A regular. All six nights since she had arrived in Enid.

He chuckled. Delicious tingles tickled nerves she didn't know existed. "That's good to hear. Thanks darlin'. I feel better knowin' you're out there. What's your favorite tune, Charity?"

Just your voice, she thought. Wildly she racked her brain. Why hadn't she thought of a tune before she dialed? She couldn't think of any song except "The Star-Spangled Banner." "Oh, my favorite . . ." Help Brain, think! " 'The Way We Were.' " She collapsed with relief.

" 'The Way We Were,' " he said, and she wished fervently it were true. "Hang on, darlin', while I put the music on." She would hang on forever. Where did she get this terrific loneliness? She hadn't even realized she was lonely until this last week. Maybe it was just leaving her friends and apartment in Tulsa, going to Enid, where she had lived with her great-aunt and uncle during three years of high school after her parents' death. The music began, and visions of Robert Redford danced into her mind. Maybe Rory Craig Runyon looked like the actor, thick blond hair, very clear blue eyes, flashing white teeth. That sexy, sensual voice could easily belong to someone who looked like Robert Redford.

And then he was back on the line, the music playing in the background.

"I'm not on the air now, darlin', the music is. There's your song. For lonely moments, moments of love."

"Thanks, Rory."

"Don't hang up. I'm lonesome tonight, darlin'. We'll say a few words on the air after the song. I'll play 'The

Way We Were' again tonight. Will you be listening later?"

"Yes." She would listen until dawn after this conversation.

"Good. I'm glad to know my audience. Charity's a beautiful name."

"It's a little old-fashioned." She didn't know what she was saying. Blue eyes danced in front of her. Blue eyes and bronzed, tanned skin. The man just had to have blue eyes. But, then again, they might be midnight-black, that lustrous darkness that was so mysterious, so . . . exciting.

"Rory . . ."

"Yes, darlin'?"

There went her heart again. Oh, my! Enid was becoming more interesting. Maybe she wouldn't rush into selling the paper and returning to Tulsa. Into the phone she said, "What . . ." She hesitated, then reminded herself the call was anonymous. All he knew was her first name. She wouldn't meet him in person, so why worry about what he thought, or about being more forward than she had ever been in her life?

"What color eyes do you have?" She blushed furiously.

"My eyes? They're light-colored."

She knew it. Blue. "I thought so. And your hair's black," she murmured dreamily, visions dancing before her.

He chuckled. "You want my hair to be black? Let me guess the color of yours. Charity. With a name like Charity . . ."

She held her breath, thankful he couldn't see her. Her mop of curls would hardly inspire a response. She looked like Miss Milkmaid of Smalltown, U.S.A.

"Charity—long, silky blond hair."

"How'd you guess!" she gasped, and her cheeks burned at the lie. Well, he was a fraction correct. It was blond.

"Ah, sweet Charity." She wriggled beneath the covers. How could a voice be so wonderful? So like a touch?

"Darlin', we're going back on the air."

He said it softly, almost apologetically. He added, "Call me again, will you?"

"Yes, Rory." In about two minutes.

"How'd you like that, Charity, darlin'?" she heard in her ear and over the radio.

"I loved it!" she said with absolute sincerity.

He chuckled. "I'm so glad! Keep in touch, darlin'. Thanks for calling me. 'Night."

" 'Nii-aight." She drew hers out just as much as he had. She didn't want to hang up the phone, to break the tenuous connection with Rory Craig Runyon. Blue eyes, black hair. Reluctantly she replaced the receiver and sank down, misty-eyed, melting beneath the covers to listen as he continued. "We're halfway into the first hour of a new day. But it's not day yet. It's still night, magic night, with stars and wind and dreams. Here's a song about the night. See if you like it."

Music wafted into the room, and Charity floated with it, carried by the sensuous voice of Rory Runyon. She replayed in her mind the way he had said her name. *Charity, darlin'*. Tingles coursed through her and she sighed. She touched her lips, then the small brown radio. " 'Night, Rory," she whispered, and closed her eyes to let Rory Craig Runyon's seductive voice lull her to sleep.

* * *

At about seven o'clock the next morning, Charity's eyes opened. She flung aside the covers, rose, stretched a body that was all rounded curves and softness, pale-skinned in the dusky room. When she raised the shades, she blinked as sunlight struck her eyes. Along with the sun she was hit in the face by the deluge of problems. Sorting through them, she decided to take one thing at a time, and the first thing was to continue helping Aunt Mattie dispense with Uncle Hubert's things.

She gazed at her plants filling the patio. They were the last remnants of her unsuccessful landscaping company. Pots of ferns, ivy, philodendrons, palms, the healthy, vigorous banana plant, airplane plants, a cactus, and dieffenbachia lined the patio across from the sturdy wooden porch swing. The swing was suspended from the ceiling and near the two old wooden rockers that had been used for years by her aunt and uncle.

Her gaze moved past the patio over the perfect yard. She knew where she had gotten her love of flowers and landscaping. It had come in the years she had lived in this house, the short time that she had learned to grow flowers, when she'd watched Uncle Hubert putter with the beds, keeping the smallest offending weed out of the neat rows of flowers. Two cardinals dipped in the birdbath, their red wings fluttering, flinging crystal drops into the still morning air. At the back of the yard crepe myrtle blooms waved, glorious pink, purple, and fuchsia banners fluttering in an armada of green bushes. Flanking them was the high top of a weathered brown board fence separating the Webster yard from Mr. O. O. Brown's. Sycamore, mulberry, hackberry, and elm trees lined his side of the fence in a tangle of green limbs.

Knowing she'd have to start the day sometime, Charity quickly dressed in faded cut-offs, a yellow knit shirt, and sneakers, brushed her unruly mop of hair, and went down the hall to the kitchen to fix breakfast.

As she set the skillet on the stove, Aunt Mattie appeared. In a blue voile dress that clung to her thin shoulders, she looked as if she were headed for church. Trifocals slipping down her nose, she smiled at Charity.

" 'Morning, Charity."

" 'Morning, Aunt Mattie. How about scrambled eggs?"

"Won't your legs get cold, dear?" Her aunt took a loaf of bread out of the breadbox.

"No, I'm fine." Charity raised her voice. "Would you like scrambled eggs?"

"As soon as we eat, I want to work on the garage. For a man who loved neatness in his yard, Hubert had so much clutter in the house."

Charity shouted, "Do you have on your hearing aid?"

Her aunt smiled. "Yes, it's lovely out this morning."

Charity took a deep breath, shouting as loudly as possible. "Aunt Mattie! Where's your hearing aid?"

"What's that, dear?"

Charity pointed at her ear. "Hearing aid!"

"Oh, that dreadful thing. It makes me feel old, like a senior citizen. I don't want to wear it. Just raise your voice a little."

Frustrated, Charity cracked three eggs into a bowl and stirred vigorously. Even though Aunt Mattie was in her eighties, she didn't care to acknowledge that she might be beyond youth. Senior citizen. In her aunt's mind that classification must be reserved for those over one hundred.

Charity poured the eggs into the skillet, trying to push aside the problems, the worries about Aunt Mattie's care, as she cooked.

After breakfast she cleaned the kitchen, then joined Aunt Mattie to tackle the garage. As they went through boxes, she found two insurance policies that should have been filed for safekeeping. She carried them to her room to place them in the dresser drawer, hesitating as she gazed at herself in the mirror. She had put on a white cotton sailor's cap to keep the dust and cobwebs out of her curls. It made her look younger. She leaned forward to brush a smudge of dust off her cheek and saw something out of the corner of her eye. A slight movement. Her gaze shifted and froze. She looked into the reflection of two black eyes at the patio window.

Her heart stopped. In the sunny glare outside, through the blur of the screen, two black eyes had peered at her, then dropped down out of sight. A window-peeper? At ten o'clock in the morning? A prowler? She had caught the barest glimpse, but there had definitely been two dark eyes at the window. Her heart thudded, and she couldn't move. She thought of Aunt Mattie in the garage. She tiptoed across the room to a window. Holding her breath, she leaned forward cautiously and peered out onto the patio.

Two

The second shock was as jolting at the first. Relief changed to anger. To pure murderous rage. A long-faced white billy goat was eating her precious banana plant. Only two leaves were left!

"Ohhhh . . . get!" she screamed, flinging up the window. "Get!"

A short white tail wagged vigorously as the goat continued to chomp with zest.

"My baby! My banana plant!" she shrieked, looking at the devastation. The palm was now only a two-inch stub in a big pot, its remains scattered over the floor. A philodendron had vanished completely. A fern lay ravaged, its feathery stems tangled and trampled on the concrete. Even the cactus was gone!

With a cry of anger filling her throat, she dashed down the hall, through the kitchen, and out onto the patio, rushing at the offending animal.

"Get out!"

When she was two feet away, the goat turned. It had horns. It fastened its beady, black eyes on her, stomped its foot, switched its tail, and lowered its head. And charged, horns first. Two little horns that suddenly looked as if he had inherited them from a Texas Longhorn.

Charity's heart went into sudden shock again. She didn't think, she ran. She grabbed the screen door handle, but it slipped out of her hands.

Screaming in fright, she dashed for the porch swing, climbed up onto an arm, and clung to the chains as the goat rammed into the swing.

The swing sailed back, then forward, and hit him in the head. He gave an angry bleat, backed up, and shook his head.

"Get out of here!"

"Baaah!"

Rage burned in Charity. Pure white-hot rage, and chicken-yellow fear. "You cannibal!"

"Baaah!"

"Aunt Mattie! Help!"

Silence. The goat switched his tail, never taking his eyes from her. She knew it wouldn't do any good to call her aunt. The hearing aid was off and Aunt Mattie was seated in a rocker in front of the garage, where there was a breeze. She would rock and look at the old albums she'd found, albums of years past with Hubert, and would probably sit there for two more hours before she stirred.

"Goat, go home."

"Baaah."

Charity wondered where the goat could have come from. She looked around. The yard was fenced, the gates closed.

"You are a cannibal, a monster, a loathsome, mean, ornery, vicious, plant-eating animal."

"Baaah."

She shifted her weight, and the swing moved beneath her. She was hot, uncomfortable, angry, and afraid of the goat. Time crept past and her legs began to ache, the soles of her feet hurt where she perched on the arm of the swing, and her hands were cramped from gripping the chain. Cautiously she lowered one foot.

The goat's head lowered at the same time, his black eyes taking aim at the swing.

She raised her foot back to her perch. "Dammit."

"Baaah."

"You are a white-bellied, mangy, carnivorous, temerarious glutton!"

"Baaah."

"Baaah yourself, Billy Whiskers! You scrawny goat. You are wicked, you have no taste, no manners, no finesse, and no looks!"

"Baaah."

She shook her fist at him. "Go! Get your four skinny legs going back to wherever you came from. You murderer. You just killed . . . five plants! Five of my precious, healthy plants are in your fat, bulging, rotten stomach!"

"Baaah."

She wiped the perspiration off her forehead, shifting her weight. He grunted, a little snort of breath, as if to remind her of his presence. She took off her sailor hat and threw it at him. It landed squarely on his head. He shook his head and the hat dropped at his feet. He bent down and began to nibble on it.

"No, dammit!"

If he heard, he ignored her.

"Goat, so help me, I'll get revenge. I'll have you put away. Leave my hat alone! It's not dessert!"

"Baaah."

She glared at him, and he returned to chewing a chunk out of the cotton brim.

"You damned billy goat." Or was it a nanny goat? Did nanny goats have horns? It had to be a male. Only a male would be that aggressive. Her legs did ache. While he chewed happily on the hat, she lowered her foot again. Carefully she lowered the other. The swing shook. The goat looked up, and then lowered his head.

She climbed back up on the arm. And stayed there for an eternity while robins and jays splashed in the bath, while bees hummed over the flowers and butterflies drifted across the yard. Shadows shortened and the sun climbed higher. Charity clung to the chain until the goat finally turned and trotted down the porch steps, across the yard, and disappeared behind the crepe myrtles.

And for the first time Charity noticed a plank missing in the board fence. The goat belonged to Mr. O. O. Brown! All her fury returned as she climbed down and eyed the devastation. Cautiously, she crossed the yard, keeping a wary eye out for the goat's return. Her heart thudded as she neared the fence. She didn't know if she could outrun the goat across the yard. The thought made her palms sweaty. Her anger was boiling like a seething volcano, ready to erupt molten rage all over Mr. O. O. Brown. She reached the fence, saw the board lying on the ground in Brown's yard, and realized there was nothing she could do about replacing it.

"Baaah."

Charity jumped violently. The goat was on the

other side of the fence, but not far away. She turned
and ran for the house, her heart pounding. As she
stepped into the kitchen, she gasped for breath, then
gazed around the empty yard, at robins fluttering in
the birdbath, butterflies still dipping over the periwinkles. But no pestiferous scraggly white face with
two beady black eyes appeared.

She was quivering with rage. She stepped back
onto the porch, scooped up her hat, and jammed it
into her curls. Stalking through the house, she
picked up a pen and paper and went out through the
front door.

As she strode down the walk she glanced at her
aunt, whose head was bent over an album. She'd only
be gone a minute. If Mr. O. O. Brown was in his office,
she would leave him a note.

Storming around the block, she headed toward the
house that backed up to Aunt Mattie's. As she
approached, she saw a white two-story house with
large shade trees in the yard and no flower beds in
sight, not even a shrub. She expected Mr. Brown to
be at work, so another shock hit her when she saw a
body filling a hammock tied between two shady syca-
mores. A very big body. Long enough to be over six
feet tall. Shoulders broad enough to stretch the white
net hammock. Her fury mounted at the sight. While
he lay indolently in the shade, the idle rich with no
worries or cares, his billy goat had demolished her
plants and held her captive on the porch swing! She
had a word or two for Mr. O. O. Brown!

She stomped up to the inert form and gazed down
in silence for a few moments at muscular forearms
sprinkled with red-gold hair; big, broad hands; a
chest covered by a blue knit shirt that clung to
muscles fit enough for a professional fighter; snug,

slim hips encased in faded, white-blue jeans; long bare feet. The face and hair were hidden by a floppy, broad-brimmed yellow straw hat.

The lazy, good-for-nothing bum. He might be rich, since he owned the radio station and wanted to buy the paper, but he was a bum nonetheless. And definitely lazy. And he owned a lethal goat.

She tapped her feet, crossed her arms over her breast, and cleared her throat.

Nothing. She cleared her throat again, louder this time.

A slight, faint wheeze reached her ears.

"Damn you," she said.

A big freckled hand reached up slowly and gripped the hat brim. The hat lowered. Thick, golden-red, sun-kissed tangled curls appeared. Beneath them a freckled forehead, then bushy red-gold, almost brown, eyebrows. Then two green eyes, startlingly green, with gold flecks in the center. A green that was summer fields and emerald fire, that brushed the heart with a promise of excitement. And eyes that were as full of devilment as the old goat's had been. Gleeful devilment that smiled and laughed and was ready for fun, that coaxed the world to drop what it was doing and come join the merriment.

She shot forth a glare, and it was deflected harmlessly off shatterproof green mirth.

The hat continued down over a crooked nose that looked as if it had come into unfortunate contact with a solid fist sometime in the past. The floppy brim brushed broad freckled cheeks, drifting down past his mouth.

A wide, well-shaped, slightly full mouth. An inviting mouth, with lips that looked . . . enticing, that matched the green eyes perfectly, that looked as if they were meant to smile or kiss . . .

She forced her gaze to follow the hat brim down over a firm jaw. A very firm jaw. No doubt he was as stubborn as the goat he owned.

"Damn you," she said again, clearly.

He grinned, and it messed up her anger. The man did have a very alluring grin. A breathtaking grin. Dimples in both cheeks even! Gleaming white teeth. Oh, my. She said sternly, "Mr. Brown."

The grin widened. "At your service, honey. Did I do something wrong?"

Oh, dear. The enemy came well-armed. His voice was husky, golden and warm like the sun. Almost as nice as Rory Craig Runyon's. Almost, but not quite as deep and resonant.

"Do you own a goat?"

"Billy?" The grin got bigger. The green eyes danced wickedly, stirring her anger into a froth.

"That damned goat!" She yanked off her hat. "Look what he did!"

Mr. Brown studied her blond curls, his gaze lowering as leisurely as his hat had, drifting down to pause on her lips—a long pause that made her draw a deep breath—lowering over her knit shirt, pausing and getting a reaction she felt and hoped didn't show, down over her legs to her feet. The silky, husky voice said, "Honey, everything looks fine to me."

"Dammit, look at my hat!"

His gaze shifted. Placing his own hat on his chest, he reached up to take hers. His hand brushed her fingers. Warm flesh touching lightly, fleetingly, yet she noticed it just as much as if she had laid her hand on the hot sidewalk. Heat singed her skin, leaving a lingering reminder of his touch.

He turned the little white sailor cap in his big fingers, studying it carefully like a jeweler squinting at a diamond, before he rendered solemn judgment. "He really ruined a priceless object."

She looked at the hat, a familiar thing that she simply wore and washed and wore again and paid little heed to. Now she saw it as if for the first time. It was frayed from a multitude of washings, from bleach, from wear. Threads had popped and stuck little tendrils into the air.

She blushed with embarrassment and anger. "All right, it's no great prize. But he did ruin some things that were prizes. He ate my banana plant!"

"He did!"

Was the man laughing at her? Her fury was growing like a prickly cactus. He looked as if he were chewing the inside of his lip.

"Honey, I'm at a disadvantage. You know me, but I don't have the pleasure."

"I'm Charity Webster. Aunt Mattie lives behind you."

"I'll be damned!" he breathed softly, his dark brows drawing together momentarily while he soberly studied her. "Charity."

"Why do you own a goat?" She couldn't resist asking.

The grin returned, a teasing, mocking grin that fueled her anger. He settled back in the hammock, placing his hands behind his head and crossing his long legs as he gazed up at her. "I don't like yard work. I don't like to mow."

"What's that have to do with a goat?"

"He eats the grass."

Oh, lordy, the man was lazy! "Look, he ate my plants!"

"I'm sorry. I'll get you some more."

"They're big and expensive. He's a menace to the world. He's mean and ornery."

"Honey, don't let my goat get your goat."

The odious man thought the whole situation was funny! "Mr. Brown—"

"Hon, it's Oregon."

"What's Oregon?"

"My name. Oregon Oliver Brown. My mother was from Oregon."

He was as weird as he was aggravating. The goat belonged to him, all right. They suited each other perfectly! She drew herself up. "There's a board missing in your fence, and that goat can just come and go as he pleases."

"Don't blame him a bit. I may come over myself."

"Mr. B—"

"Oregon."

"Are you going to fix your fence?"

"Sure thing." He fanned himself with his hat.

"When?"

"Honey, you do get worked up about little things. Take life easy. I'm sorry about your uncle. I guess you've been here since the funeral."

"That's right. The flowers you sent were nice."

"Your aunt's a sweet little lady."

"That goat could do her in, you know."

"Billy wouldn't harm a flea."

"Oh, ho! Little do you know about your damned old goat!"

His eyes became thoughtful. "Did Billy hurt you?"

"No." She felt the fiery blush flood her cheeks, a telltale giveaway that something had happened between her and the goat. And Mr. Odious Oregon Oliver Brown wasn't going to let it pass unnoticed.

"He did do something to you!" He stopped fanning.

"That's not important. What's important are my plants."

"Hon, what did Billy do to you? He's so harmless. Did he bite you?" Again his gaze drifted slowly down over her thighs, her long bare legs, returning just as leisurely to her burning face. "You sure look all right."

"No, he didn't bite me! I'd just as soon not discuss my encounter with your goat. I want restitution and the fence fixed."

"I'll restitute whatever you want," he drawled in his sexy, husky voice, making it sound like the most suggestive thing she had heard in ages. And, aggravating her further, he added, "And I promised to fix the fence."

"When?"

"You do worry, don't you?" He was trampling her patience into the dust, mangling it as Billy had her plants.

"It's not a little thing! He could kill Aunt Mattie!"

"Billy?" Dark eyebrows shot up, and gleeful, wicked green devils capered wildly. "Now I have to know. What did Billy do to you?"

"If you must know—he chased me up onto the porch swing and kept me there for an hour!"

Oregon Brown sat up swiftly, plopping his bare feet on the ground, resting his elbows on his knees, bending his head down while he rubbed a broad hand across the back of his freckled neck below a thick brush of golden-red curls. And she knew he was hiding his laughter.

She was seething with rage. That damned goat had scared the wits out of her, kept her pinned on the swing for an hour, and his owner thought the whole episode was hilarious. She wanted to fling every one of her flowerpots at Oregon Brown.

"It's not funny, Mr. Brown."

He didn't answer, but the freckled hand on his neck rubbed faster. "I know," finally came out, muffled from his downturned head.

"Isn't it against the law to have a goat in town?"

"I have a permit."

"A goat permit?"

He raised his head. His lips were pressed tightly together, the corners of his mouth twitched, his cheeks were red, and his green eyes left no doubt whatsoever that Mr. Oregon Brown was about to split his sides with laughter.

He controlled it. The effort must have been stupendous. He flicked a glance at her and his lips tightened some more.

"How could you get a goat permit?"

"Because . . ." He paused and tried to keep his voice steady. "I'm not raising livestock. I have a live lawn mower."

She glanced at the bare yard. "It looks like a goat lives here," she said acidly, and his lips pursed, the dimples appearing in spite of his clamped jaw, and infuriating crinkles fanning out from his eyes. Laugh lines!

After a second he said, "Maybe I'd better come around and view the damage."

"That's fine, but first will you put the board in place on the fence so he can't come back?"

Oregon Brown stood up. Even barefoot he towered over her. She felt as if she were standing next to a Mack truck—except his lower half tapered down to such narrow hips. He had a massive chest and powerful arms that bulged with muscle. How had anyone who was so lazy developed such a set of muscles? It was like discovering that a sloth had the muscles of a tiger. The man must have moments when he moved. He took her arm. "Come on, honey. Let's get you acquainted with Billy."

She dug in her heels. "No! I don't want to see that goat again!"

"He's gentle as a lamb. Come on." Reluctantly she followed him around the house. There were tall shade trees and little else. The green grass was clipped close to the ground. There wasn't a stick of vegetation other than the short grass and tall trees and a wide elm stump by the gate. The yard looked neat, but not too appealing.

They reached the gate and he started to unfasten the black iron hinge.

"That goat doesn't like me."

"Billy loves you, I'm sure. How could he resist?"

Now, what did he mean by that remark? Her anger was swiftly transforming into fear. She did not care for Billy and she was sure the feeling was mutual. Very mutual.

Oregon Brown held the gate open, and when she brushed past him she caught a whiff of a clean male scent. But the enticing scent was forgotten when she entered the yard. Billy was chomping grass, his beady eyes focused on the ground. Oregon called, "Hey, Billy."

The goat raised its head, studied them a moment, and put its head down in its charging position.

"Oh, oh!" Charity started to back up. Suddenly the goat started running toward her, head down. Hard arms scooped her up against a chest shaking with laughter.

"We'd better get you out of here." Oregon stepped

through the gate and kicked it shut, dropping the latch in place. "I'll be hornswoggled. He doesn't like you. Imagine that!" Oregon held her close, his wicked, merry eyes inches away, his full lips inches away. One of her arms was wound around his very warm, very solid neck, the other hand resting lightly against his broad chest.

She was trapped by his green-gold eyes, like green fields with golden sunlight sprinkled in them. Her heart began drumming with excitement.

"Billy just became a whole lot more valuable," Oregon said in a husky voice that drew attention from every nerve in her body.

"Now, look," she said, but her own voice was weak.

"I am looking, and I can't resist." He leaned forward the few inches necessary to brush her lips with his. It was the lightest breath of a touch, a whisper of warm flesh, of full, firm lips that barely touched, left, then returned swiftly to linger, to dally, to start a molten current flowing through her veins. His arms tightened, crushing her to his broad warm chest. He smelled so good, so clean, like morning air after a rain. His lips were like velvet, as his tongue explored, touching hers, reveling in the moist warmth, tracing the inside of her lips to stir a response from her. For one full minute Charity Webster forgot everything in the whole world except strong arms, and enticing male scent, and sensuous, hot kisses.

Oregon walked a few steps and propped one bare foot on the tree stump, setting her on his thigh, which felt as firm beneath her rounded bottom as an iron bench. He wrapped both arms around her and crushed her softness to him, and then really kissed her. The dallying changed into a hot, thrusting demand, a searching that brought an instant response, that blanked out memory and logic from Charity's brain.

It was Charity's first kiss in too long, and it was as devastating as a tidal wave. Swamped and buffeted, she clung in a daze to Oregon Brown.

The world stopped turning, hung in the universe, wobbled crazily, went widdershins, then finally righted and settled in its normal course. Memory returned to Charity. Along with it came shock, then anger. She twisted violently, tearing her lips from his. "Put me down this instant. Dammit, I've had it with you, Oregon Brown! Don't kiss me." She wriggled off his leg and slipped to the ground, but his arms still held her waist and his propped-up leg pressed against her hip.

"You do swear a lot, Miss Charity Jane."

Another shock. "How did you know my name is Jane?"

Three

"And how'd you know it's 'Miss'?" she couldn't resist asking, and wished fervently that she didn't sound so breathless. And wished he would move his leg, his arms, just not stand so close.

"Your Aunt Mattie and Uncle Hubert have told me about you in great, glowing terms, about your business, your astute . . . mind, the cute little things you did in high school, how you lived with an Aunt Ziza before you came to stay with them, your breakup with Ted Farnsworth. I've listened to your letters . . ."

"Oh, no!" The day had started badly. With Oregon Brown's words it went downhill like an avalanche.

"Oh, yes. I know all about Theodore Farnsworth and . . . what was the name of the guy you dated three times after you broke up with Farnsworth? Brogan?"

"Dammit!" She gasped for breath. "That is none of your business any more than kissing me is!"

He grinned, that wide, infuriating grin that was as inviting as the yellow brick road. Well, she was immune to that grin. Absolutely. Inoculated by fury, rage, and anger.

He tilted her chin up. She tried to jerk away, but his fingers tightened on her jaw. "I kissed you because you needed to be kissed. I've heard the letters about how you're swearing off men, how terrible Farnsworth was, about how you decided to swear off men after Brogan . . ."

She managed to glare at him, but what was the matter with her heart, her lungs, her nerves? Her heart was thumping wildly, her lungs wouldn't function, and her nerves were overfunctioning because of a freckled-faced, tousled-headed, mulish man! "You keep out of my life!" she snapped.

"It's too interesting, hon," he said with maddening cheer. "You're very particular about men, you know that?"

"That's enough!"

He took hold of one of her hands before she could snatch it away. "Who's the current guy?"

"That's none of your business!" He was studying her hand as if he had never seen one in his life. One of his big fingers traced up and down her small, slender ones, trailing lightly between them, sending fiery tingles spreading upward that were more intense than such a light touch warranted. "I'll have to have a talk with Aunt Mattie about my letters," she added.

"Don't worry your sweet aunt." His eyes caught and held hers. "It's been fun to hear them. You have a nice sense of the ridiculous. Too much humor for Mr. Farnsworth. That was good riddance. Brogan, too."

Odious Oregon Oliver Brown. He really was unbelievably odious. As irritating as his goat. "You and Billy belong together. What a perfect pair!"

He grinned and twisted a golden curl around his finger. "Such blond curls. Who has the curliest hair?"

"I don't really care!"

"Let's put our heads together and see." He leaned forward until his forehead touched hers and ran his big hand over the tops of their heads. Harmless, except his eyes were absorbing her and his lips were a fraction of an inch away. Too, too close. Then they weren't away at all. They brushed hers, melded with hers, and his bold tongue played havoc with her nerves.

This time she recovered faster, but the residual effect went deeper. Her mouth tingled and ached for more, but what did her lips know about anything?

He laughed and his dimples showed, twin indentations that were mirth and fun. The pesky man was "danger" in big red letters!

"I'll nail up the fence," he said, "then come over and look at the damage."

"You do that." His arms dropped away and she felt degrees cooler. She stomped off down the street, but from her head to her heels, the back of her tingled with an irresistible tug. She fought it past one more house, to the corner, then she had to yield. She looked back. He stood facing her, his muscled arms folded over his broad chest, grinning from freckled ear to freckled ear, sunshine creating a nimbus of red-gold curls around his head. He waved.

Charity gritted her teeth and marched around the corner. She hated the thought of selling Uncle Hubert's paper to such a lazy, ornery man. A man who owned a goat so he wouldn't have to mow. Who lazed in a hammock at eleven in the morning. A man whose kiss was the devil's own temptation!

Now, why had she thought that? His kisses weren't temptation. No. She was just lonesome. They merely *seemed* better than Ted's or Hank Brogan's—Charity stopped in her tracks, then clamped her jaw shut until it ached. They merely *seemed* better because it had been so long since anyone had kissed her. It was loneliness. The same dreadful loneliness that made Rory Craig Runyon's voice sound so sexy, so tempting. She chewed on her lip. Mr. O. O. Brown was obnoxious! Probably the only reason the old goat didn't attack Brown was because the man was as big as a tank. The goat knew when he had met his match. Billy goat. What a name. No originality at all!

As she turned the next corner, she glanced overhead and saw gray clouds darkening the day, gathering, rolling swiftly across the sky while the wind blew in fierce gusts. They needed rain, but the clouds might blow right over without spilling a drop. Too bad a storm hadn't come early enough to keep Billy in his own backyard!

She marched up the walk; Aunt Mattie wasn't in sight. She found her aunt in the kitchen.

"Aunt Mattie," she shouted.

"Oh, dear, what's wrong?"

"Oh, you have on your hearing aid. Aunt Mattie, Mr. Brown will be over shortly. His goat got into our yard and ate up my plants this morning."

"Billy did?"

Charity felt a sinking feeling. "You know Billy?"

"That sweet little goat. Isn't he cute? Almost like a puppy."

Charity wanted to grind her teeth. "Aunt Mattie, that goat is mean as hel——as heck."

"Billy? He wouldn't harm a fly. You should've seen the way he let Hubert feed him little bites of cookies. Oregon took a board out of the fence so Billy could come over. Hubert would rock and Billy would stand on the patio, wagging his little tail, waiting for Hubert to break off a bite and hold it out. Then Billy would whisk it out of Hubert's hand so cutely." She sniffed and wiped her eyes while Charity wondered if O. O. Brown had two goats.

"It was Billy?"

"Yes. You'll love him."

"I don't believe so. Aunt Mattie, what does Mr. Brown do, besides owning the radio station?"

"He inherited his father's wheat land—there's oil on it. He has a man to manage the farm."

"I vaguely remember the Browns when I lived here during high school, but I don't remember Oregon Brown."

"Oh, no, dear. He's older than you. Oregon is thirty-two, and when you were in high school, he was already out of college. He'd moved to Virginia and was working on the *Washington Post*. He came back here after his parents' death. He's been here about six months now. He goes to the same church we do. You'll see him when we go."

Charity's mind was on something else. So he did know how to work. Journalism. No wonder he wanted the paper. "Aunt Mattie, please don't read my letters to Oregon Brown."

Aunt Mattie laughed. "Your letters are interesting, and Oregon used to come sit on the patio with us and I'd read your latest letter."

The doorbell interrupted Charity's reply about the

letters. "That's probably Mr. Brown," she said. For one fleeting moment she thought of his green eyes and wished she had brushed her hair and washed her face. Ridiculous. She compressed her lips and walked to the door and opened it.

The sight of Oregon Brown made her heart jump in the most absurd manner. She had been too long without kisses and hugs and dates, and her heart, her lips, her entire body didn't understand that she didn't want to notice the man standing before her. Down to her most insignificant little nerve, she noticed Oregon Brown. Noticed and quivered like willow branches in the summer wind. "You've already hammered that board in place?" she asked suspiciously.

"It fits on. I used to keep it off so Billy could come see your uncle Hubert. Wind blew it off last night." He leaned close to her throat and sniffed.

She looked down at his freckled cheek, the thick copper-colored lashes. His breath tickled her throat, and she had to fight an urge to jump back. "What are you doing?"

"I thought maybe it was your perfume that Billy didn't like. Mmmm, he couldn't dislike that fragrance. What is it?" He straightened.

Why did she suspect everything he said or did? Maybe it was the ever-present laughter in his eyes, as if he found her a constant source of amusement. She said, "It's Chloe. Billy just doesn't like me. He wasn't close enough to smell my perfume."

"Let's go look at the disaster area."

"Aunt Mattie!" she called as she led the way. "I don't know where she is. She was just here." When they reached the patio, Charity waved her arm in a sweeping gesture. "There!"

He looked at the plants, the littered floor. His gaze shifted to the porch swing, drifting up the chain fastened to the ceiling, and his lips pursed again. His brow furrowed, and her anger shot up accordingly. "I'd like to see you hang up there an hour!" The moment she said it she wished she could take it back. Oregon Brown would never be treed by a goat. And she knew it made his amusement deepen.

His eyes met hers. "I'll pay for everything." He reached into a back pocket and withdrew a pencil and note pad. "Let's sit down and you list them off."

She didn't want to sit down with Oregon Brown, but she perched on the swing anyway. When he settled beside her, his broad shoulder touching hers lightly, she had a ridiculous urge to jump up and move. Determined not to be bothered by the man, she studied her wrecked greenery instead of him. But it was so difficult to ignore his fresh scent, the jean-clad knee near hers, and his big hands moving close to her.

She took a deep breath and said, "There's a philodendron, my banana plant, which was five—" Forgetting her resolve not to look at him, she turned and glared accusingly at Oregon. The hint of longing in his eyes startled her, and she instantly lost her train of thought.

He waited for a moment, then his brows arched questioningly. "Yes?"

He had the most enticing mouth, a beautifully shaped upper lip and slightly full lower lip. He smiled, and she realized he had asked her a question.

"You have a five-year-old banana plant?" he prompted.

"No, I don't know how old it was! What difference does its age make?"

Even though his expression remained impassive, she heard the suppressed laughter in his voice. "Charity, you said you had a banana plant that was five. I presumed you meant five years old."

She clenched her jaw. "It was five feet tall."

"Oh! Five feet tall. You didn't say that."

Damn the man. He was every bit as odious now as he had been earlier! She wished she knew how to stop a blush. His eyes were twinkling, but then the twinkle disappeared, replaced by a solemn look. Something was happening between them. He focused on her intently, sitting absolutely still. The air fairly crackled between them, and then it was gone. There was no air to breathe. She couldn't get the smallest breath. She couldn't talk. She couldn't pull her gaze away from Oregon Brown's. And he seemed to be suffering the same malady.

Only, he could move. He leaned over and kissed her. It was a light, questing kiss, his lips brushed hers, his knee barely pressed hers, and his hands didn't touch her. Again he brushed her lips with his, and it was so delectable! Her heart was thudding as his mouth settled on hers, parting her lips sweetly, and his tongue probed inside.

Somewhere in the depths of her being she felt the tension that gripped her tighten its hold. It became too constricting to bear. She struggled to gather her wits, vaguely aware that they weren't alone, that Mattie might appear any minute.

She straightened and leaned back. Oregon's mouth was parted from their kiss, and his lids were drooping over his blazing eyes. "Let's stick to the plants," she said, her voice a breathy whisper.

"Plants?"

She knew he was about to reach for her again. And

she knew that part of her wanted him to, that she might not be able to resist. She stood up and crossed the patio to the plants. Her thumping heart didn't seem to realize she had moved away from the source of trouble. When she turned to look at Oregon, her pulse raced just as rapidly as before.

"He ate a five-foot banana plant." She could barely say the words. Oregon sat back, one foot on his knee, one arm stretched on the back of the swing. He was looking at her with such intensity she felt as if she were the first and only woman he had ever desired. With an effort she tore her gaze away. "You're not taking notes," she said.

"No, I forgot all about notes," he answered in a husky voice that was as sexy as his kiss.

"Well, write it down!" She risked looking at him.

One corner of his mouth lifted in a crooked grin that showed off his dimples and aggravated her. He looked so damned smug! As if he knew his kisses or his voice or his eyes could turn her knees to jelly. She raised her chin, and his grin widened.

"Will you stop that!" she snapped, then instantly wished she hadn't lost control. They were locked in a contest and he had just scored.

In a sensual, suggestive drawl that shook her to her toes, he asked, "Stop what?"

"Just write down the plants Billy ate." She ground out the words, hating the blush that burned her cheeks. She turned with determination to study another destroyed plant. "One palm, very healthy and very large."

"You like plants, don't you?"

"These were left from my landscaping business."

"Why did you have tropical plants in a landscape company?"

She tried to talk without looking at him, and it felt ridiculous. "People wanted me to do their patios, and occasionally I'd provide plants inside a house or business."

"You had a run of bad luck last summer. Hubert told me about the employee who lost control of the mower and drove through the plate-glass window and lobby of a building."

"Insurance covered most of that one, but they canceled the policy when another employee hit a parked car with a mower," she said to the stub of the palm. Her pulse was almost down to normal. She faced him. He smiled, and it wasn't as earthshaking as she had feared. It was pleasant, downright pleasant to look at Oregon Brown!

"Where'd you find the employees?"

She shrugged. "I had a hard time keeping any. They'd come and go. That was the biggest problem. Another one drove a mower into the lake in front of the Tower Center complex, and that really cost me. I had to pay for two more ride-on mowers and the damaged cars." She looked back at her plants. "Well, here's what's left of the fern. I guess it'll come out again and survive."

He made a note. "One fern."

"And he ate a cactus! How could he chew up a cactus?"

"Billy can crunch down most anything that doesn't get him first," Oregon said with an engaging grin. "What else?"

"As I said before, he ate my philodendron, but don't worry about it. I can replace it easily." Suddenly she felt silly for making such an issue of five plants. To Oregon, who probably had seen whole wheat farms destroyed by hail, it must be absolutely absurd.

Oregon wrote it down anyway. "Anything else?"

"No, that's all. The plants were all I had left from my business, and somehow, as long as I had them, I felt as if I still had part of my business, as if I could start again." She shook her head. "I guess that sounds silly."

"Are you going to start over?"

"I'd like to, but I don't think I can for a long time." She didn't add the reason, but she had a suspicion Oregon Brown had already been informed about her debts to the last penny. She had written detailed letters to Uncle Hubert.

"Are you going to stay in Enid a while?"

"Yes. I have to decide what to do about Aunt Mattie. You know, now that I've calmed down, the whole thing doesn't seem that important. I don't need a five-foot banana plant or a palm tree. Maybe I wanted something that was mine to take care of. Just forget it, Oregon."

He rose, a coordinated unfolding of his big frame that made her feel as if the patio had suddenly shrunk and he was filling it completely. "It's nothing," he said easily. "Hereafter I'll keep Billy home. I can't imagine why he doesn't like you. Shows a definite lack of intelligence."

She smiled. "Thanks." Now, why couldn't Oregon be nice like that all the time? Just pleasant, instead of ornery and teasing and disturbing!

"I'll just go home this way. See you later."

He sauntered across the yard, and it was difficult to stop watching him. She went to the kitchen, and when she looked out the window he had disappeared. Deciding that, for her own peace of mind, she should think about anything but him, she started cleaning the kitchen cabinets, changing shelf paper that hadn't been changed in years, and thought about Rory Runyon. An idea came to her and sent her into her room to make a list of song titles that she would request just to hear them repeated in Rory Runyon's husky voice.

That night, hours after Mattie had gone to bed, Charity bathed, pulled on a cotton nightie, and climbed into bed with the list of songs. At the same time that the familiar music started, a flash of lightning briefly illuminated the room. Outside a steady patter of raindrops was beating on the sloping patio roof. Charity settled against the pillows, closing her eyes to conjure up an image of Tom Selleck while she listened to the radio.

"Here we are again," Rory Runyon said. "It's 'Nighttime,' coming to you from Station KKZF with songs for midnight, soft, lulling music to put you in the mood. Have you been outside? There are rain clouds over us tonight, a gentle spring rain. Snuggle up, darlin'. We'll listen to music while raindrops pitter-pat on the windows."

Oh, how Charity wanted to snuggle up! His voice wrapped its shaggy warmth around her, enveloping her.

"Darlin' . . ." Pause. Charity opened her eyes and looked at the radio. Then, in a lazy baritone voice, so sexy she quivered from shoulder to knee, Rory continued. "This song is for you, darlin', just you." Didn't she wish! "Here's your song, darlin'. Here's 'Just You and Me.' "

She sank down, pulling the soft sheet to her chin while she listened to the music and wondered about Rory Runyon. Was he married? Did he have a woman in his life? Where did he live? She would ask Oregon Brown. Rory worked for Oregon, and surely Oregon would know whether the man was married or not. What a voice he had! "Just You and Me." Oh, to hear him say it again! Oregon had a sexy voice, too, but his personality ruined the effect. She did not want to think about Oregon Brown. She refused to think about him. Her lips tingled. She pressed them together, squeezed her eyes closed, and waited. The record finally finished.

" 'Just You and Me,' darlin'." Rory said. "There it is for you alone." His voice raised a fraction. "Here's something special—Captain Nemo's Fudge Bars. Fresh, delicious chocolate, melt-in-your mouth bites. I mean to tell you, these are mouth-waterin', oozy"— his voice lowered with every word, and every word wafted over Charity's simmering nerves, causing tremors—"sweet fudge, the thick, dark fudge like Momma used to make. Did you like to lick the pan?"

"Yes," Charity said, agonizing over his drawling pronunciation.

"Oh, so did I. Scrape a little bit of thick fu-udge"— and "fudge" became a two-syllable, drawn-out word that made Charity take a long, deep breath—"off the pan and lick the last drop off the spoon. Well, I'll tell you what. If you like fudge, get some Captain Nemo Fudge Bars and unwrap the silver paper to bite off a chunk and s-a-v-o-r it"—Charity savored his voice, wriggling her hips unconsciously and running the tip of her tongue over her dry lips—"hold it in your mouth and just let it melt. That soft, creamy rich chocolate, so thick. Let it melt. You'll agree Captain Nemo's Fudge Bars are the most delicious candy you've tasted. Try some soon, y'hear? Listen to that rain. Makes you want to curl up where it's warm and dry, doesn't it?" Charity wanted to curl up with Rory Runyon.

"Here's a song for a rainy night, for you, darlin'," he said in a voice like a distant rumble of thunder. "Here's 'I've Got Love on My Mind.' "

Charity wiggled her toes and wondered what Rory was wearing, what kind of car he drove. Again she went over his talk of the past few minutes, the way he said certain words that made them sensuous, suggestive, so sexy! At the same time she felt ridiculous. Never in her life had she acted so silly or felt so lonesome. Maybe it was everything rolled together—being away from home, away from her friends, the worries, the loss of her business. Her attention returned to the radio as Rory came on to ask for requests. Charity reached for the phone and dialed, only to receive a busy signal.

Aggravated, she listened to a young girl's giggly voice talk to Rory Runyon.

"Rory, this is—" The girl giggled and finally gasped, "Gloria!"

"Hi, there, Gloria. Do you listen to 'Nighttime' often?"

More giggles. Charity groaned. Gloria's squeaky voice said, "I listen every night you're on."

"Do you, really? My goodness, what a fan you are! What would you like to hear tonight?"

Charity rolled her eyes while she listened to giggles, but she did notice Rory's voice had raised from the intimate, husky level and he wasn't using "darlin'." The man had some sense as well as a sexy voice. Gloria giggled and gasped as she answered, "I'd like, 'Mean Mr. Mustard.' "

" 'Mean Mr. Mustard' it is!" Rory laughed softly. "Here he is, just for Gloria."

Disgusted, Charity threw back the covers and went to the kitchen to get a drink of water. As she stood at the kitchen sink, lightning flashed and she saw Oregon Brown's dark house. Oregon Brown. For an instant she remembered his kisses and felt as if an invisible bolt of lightning had streaked through the stormy sky and struck her. An electric jolt sizzled in her; then she shook her head to clear away the memory. The man could kiss. No doubt about it.

She hurried back to the bedroom and climbed into bed in time to hear the end of "Mean Mr. Mustard," and Gloria's final giggles. Then Rory's velvety voice glided like thick fog into the room.

Charity continued to listen and wasn't able to call in a request until the last half hour of the program. Finally she breathed ecstatically into the phone, "Rory, this is Charity."

"Charity, darlin'."

Oh, my! A dreamy sensation swirled in her. "I thought you'd never call," he continued. "Just tune in, darlin'?"

"No. The line was busy before."

"You've listened since the beginning?" He sounded so satisfied! What difference would it make to him whether she listened or not?

"I've listened from the very first. Since you played 'Just You and Me.' "

"Good! What would you like to hear now?"

Ahhh. Even though she knew it from memory, she held the list beneath the red glow of the radio. It was a toss-up between "You Do Something to Me," and "You're My Thrill." She chose "You're My Thrill," and put heart and soul into it when she said it to him. "Rory, 'You're My Thrill.' " Her heart thudded violently, and she blushed.

" 'You're My Thrill,' " darlin'," he repeated, only he changed the emphasis to "my". "Don't go 'way."

The music came on, an old instrumental song, then faded into the background as Rory said, "Darlin', I've been waiting for your call."

She was sure he said that to everyone. Everyone maybe except the gigglers and kids like Gloria. But she loved it anyway and sighed with satisfaction. "I've tried, Rory."

"I wish we were together. Listen to the rain, darlin'. I'd like to be beside you and we'd listen to the rain and I'd hold you." His voice dropped to a raspy purr. "Hold you and kiss you."

"Oh, you don't know me! You might feel differently if we met."

"We're going to have to meet soon, darlin'. Real soon."

"Rory, are you married?" The words came out as if of their own volition. Why had she asked him that? She sat up, burning with embarrassment.

"No, darlin', I'm not married. You're not either, are you?"

"No. I didn't mean to get so personal, but all I know is a voice. I get curious. . . ."

"Ask away, darlin'. I'll answer anything you want to know," he said in such intimate, suggestive tones that she blanked out completely. Not one question came to mind.

"No questions, darlin'?" He chuckled softly. She nestled in the soft, warm sheets and let his voice nuzzle her, sending her senses into a trembling longing that wiped out logical thought.

She listened in silence to the music, then Rory said, "Darlin', we're going back on the air and it's time to close. Call me tomorrow night, will you?"

"Oh, yes!"

"I'll think of you when I go home tonight. Sleep well, darlin'."

How could she sleep after that! She hung up the phone and listened to him say good night to her on the air, then play his last song and close. It was an hour before she drifted to sleep, and then she dreamed about green-gold eyes and aggravating dimples.

The next day, Tuesday, she woke to a sunny morning and dressed again in cut-offs and a blue T-shirt. Forgetting about Oregon and the plants, she helped Mattie clean out Uncle Hubert's desk and dresser, unaware of the change in the weather as the morning went on. Gray clouds appeared on the horizon and gradually moved overhead, bringing rumbles of thunder and the threat of more rain. About eleven o'clock the doorbell rang. Charity answered to find a uniformed man holding a large basket of philodendron. He peered at her over it. "Are you Miss Webster?"

"Yes," she answered. Beyond him she saw a truck with "Smith's Flowers" painted on the side.

"Well, I'm supposed to deliver some plants. Where do you want them?"

"Around the back, on the patio, please. I'll take this one."

"Sure." He handed over the basket and sauntered to the truck. Charity explained to Aunt Mattie and went out to the patio to tell the man where to set the plants. And discovered that Oregon had doubled the replacement. When the man had finished and left, Charity stood on the porch with two six-foot banana plants, two potted palms, two baskets of philodendron, one tall, spiky cactus and one short cactus, three kinds of ferns, two pots of ivy, a new airplane plant, and another dieffenbachia. As she surveyed the greenery, a mixture of emotions churned in her. She was embarrassed that she had demanded Oregon replace what Billy had destroyed, she was aggravated at his generosity, and she loved the plants. While she mulled it over, Aunt Mattie called to her, "Charity, here's Oregon."

With a startled glance at her cut-offs and T-shirt, she turned to the back door as it opened and he appeared. Her heart jumped ridiculously over the big smile he flashed at her. Dressed in a blue plaid cotton shirt and faded jeans, he was as forceful as ever. "I see the plants arrived," he said.

"Thanks, but you went beyond the call of duty. I feel silly for getting so angry about a bunch of plants."

He shrugged and strolled over to one of the banana plants, measuring its height against his shoulder. "That's okay. I owed them to you."

"Not twice as many! You sent me more than Billy ate."

He looked at her, and her body tingled from her head to her toes. "That's what I wanted to do."

End of subject. "Well, thank you. I love them!"

"Good." He walked back to her and braced one hand against the wall and leaned over her. "What else do you love besides plants, Charity Jane?"

"You ought to know, you've heard all the letters!" she snapped, losing the friendly warmth she had felt for about one minute toward Oregon. She wanted to run, but he had her blocked between the wall, the banana plants, his arm, and his body. Thunder rumbled and a flash of lightning crackled across the cloudy sky. To Charity's relief, the back door opened and Aunt Mattie appeared with a chilled pitcher of lemonade, ice cubes rattling and clinking as she struggled through the door. Oregon relieved her of the pitcher instantly, stretching his long arm over Charity's head to hold the door.

"It's almost lunch time," Aunt Mattie said, "so I fixed some sandwiches."

Oregon grinned while Charity groaned inwardly. She didn't want to have lunch with him. A gust of wind whipped across the patio, bringing cooler air that smelled like rain.

"Oh, my." Aunt Mattie looked up. "Maybe we'll have to eat inside."

"I think so." Oregon squinted at the overcast sky. "Storm's coming up fast."

Another gust buffeted them, flinging gritty dust against Charity's bare legs. At the end of the patio, the dieffenbachia bent dangerously beneath the onslaught.

"Oh, the plants!" Charity cried. "You two go inside. I'll take in the ones that can't stand the wind."

While Oregon held the door for Aunt Mattie and disappeared behind her, Charity picked up a flowerpot and carried it to her room.

When she turned to leave the bedroom, she almost collided with Oregon and a large potted palm. He smiled through the fronds. "Thought I'd help."

"Thanks."

He was blocking her path, and slowly lowered the plant and looked around. "This is your bedroom."

A tingle, definitely unwanted, slipped down her back. He had a sexy, vibrant voice. It didn't match the rest of him. In fairness, she realized that was a harsh judgment. If they had met under other circumstances, she might not have felt that way at all. His green eyes could be so inviting!

"Yes, it is," she said coolly. "Will you step aside, please? My plants will get ruined."

"Oh, sure. Just curious about where you sleep."

He could fill the most innocuous statement with such innuendo. She hurried outside, glad to be on the cool patio. Black clouds were boiling overhead, darkening the day to dusk. Wind gusts swept against the house, spattering big, cold drops of rain. She picked up another pot. Large hands took it from her. "I'll get these. Go inside; you'll get wet."

"I won't melt."

He grinned, and his gaze drifted down. "Guess you won't at that."

She clamped her jaw closed and grabbed another plant. He held the door while balancing a huge potted palm. They just set the plants down in the kitchen, but when Charity turned back to the porch, it was being drenched by the driving gray rain. Determined to save the remaining plants, she braved the cold water and snatched up two more pots.

One more trip outside and they were through. And soaked thoroughly. As they stood dripping on the kitchen floor, she looked at Oregon. He was staring at her, and his heated gaze slowly lowered over her face, her neck, her shoulders, then paused.

And she realized her wet shirt was plastered to her, molding the full, soft curves of her breasts and revealing her hardened nipples.

His eyes flicked up to hers, and he smiled lazily. She blushed furiously, certain he could feel the heat.

"I'll go change," she said.

"Here, Oregon." Aunt Mattie appeared from the hallway. "I brought you a towel. Give me your shirt and I'll put it in the dryer."

"Sure thing."

Charity fled the kitchen as if the demons of hell were after her. She didn't want to stand there and watch Oregon Brown take off his shirt. She hoped the mere thought didn't disable her heart.

She closed the bedroom door, but she couldn't shut out the feeling of invasion. Oregon Brown's aura lingered in the room, big and male and overwhelming.

She changed quickly into jeans, a white shirt, and sandals. She brushed her hair and applied a little blush, a dab of perfume. And braced herself for the next encounter as she stepped into the kitchen.

She didn't brace enough. Aunt Mattie and Oregon were sitting at the kitchen table, her aunt's back to the door and Oregon facing it. He had a small blue towel thrown carelessly across his shoulders with the ends draping over his chest, but it didn't hide his golden, freckled bare shoulders, the soft, curly red-gold fuzz that covered his impressive chest and tapered slightly to disappear beneath the low-slung damp jeans. When he saw her, he stood up in a sensuous movement that was filled with masculine grace.

He held out a chair while his languorous appraisal of her fouled up her brain. The room was suffocatingly hot; the walls were closing in. He was just so damned big and male and fit. There wasn't anywhere to look. She didn't want to meet his amused, knowing eyes. She didn't want to gaze at his powerful, sexy body—and it was so sexy! And she didn't want to ignore him, because it would reveal to him how disturbed she was. Another muddle brought on by Oregon Brown! She opted to look into his eyes and immediately wished she hadn't. He was very obviously amused.

The chair he had pulled out was next to his. Why

hadn't he been so damned polite yesterday when he was stretched in his hammock? She didn't want to sit by him, but she wasn't going to let the man scare her. So she took the chair he offered.

As soon as she sat down, he shifted his chair away. The relief she felt was short-lived, because in two seconds she realized that he had moved so that he was in her view. He could look at her and it would be natural for her to look back at him. And if he stretched out his legs, they would touch hers.

"Now we can eat," Aunt Mattie said, oblivious of the broad bare chest that made Charity sure she couldn't swallow one bite. That towel was so tiny.

"Have a tuna sandwich, Charity. The wheat-bread sandwiches are tuna and the white-bread sandwiches are pimento cheese."

Charity reached for the plate. Just as her fingers closed on it, lightning crackled and an explosion reverberated in the storm. The kitchen lights blinked off.

Four

Outside something crackled. Oregon rose and peered out the back door. He stepped outside, then returned swiftly. "Lightning hit the transformer. I'll call the fire department."

While Charity watched the blaze, the orange flames leaping up in spite of the rain, Oregon phoned the fire department, then tried in vain to get the electric company.

Within minutes the fire was over, but Oregon still couldn't get through to the electric company. He stood at the phone with his back to the room, and Charity stared without thinking at the splash of freckles over his golden shoulders, at his smooth, muscled back. He turned around, caught her staring, and grinned.

Blushing, she sat down at the table. "Don't you want to eat and call them later?"

He hung up the phone. "I think I'll do that." Something thoughtful in his tone made her look sharply at him, but his expression was bland and he sat down. He accepted the plate of sandwiches, took one of each kind, then asked Aunt Mattie, "Do you have a freezer?"

"Just the refrigerator-freezer."

"Good. I think you're going to be without electricity for some time."

Charity had been about to take a bite from her sandwich, but she set it down. "Why do you think so?"

"Because I can't get the electric company. I've been through this before. It probably means the electricity is off other places in town. They repair in the order of the calls they get."

He took a bite of his sandwich. She had an uneasy feeling.

"If you'd like," he said to Aunt Mattie, "you can stay at my house until your electricity comes on."

Charity choked on a piece of tuna. She covered her mouth and tried to clear her throat. When she recovered, she asked, "What makes you think you have electricity? You're on the same block."

He looked too satisfied. "Same block, but a different transformer."

Aunt Mattie answered, serenely unaware of undercurrents, "Thank you, Oregon. You're a nice young man, but we'll stay here. We don't need lights."

Charity's mind was clipping along above the speed limit. Aunt Mattie went down with the sun. She didn't need electricity after dark, but no electricity—no radio! Charity would miss Rory Craig Runyon. And he was becoming important in her life. All day she wrestled with problems, every evening she fought loneliness. Rory Runyon was the bright moment in her life. She debated. As aggravating as Oregon Brown was, Rory Runyon was delightful.

"I won't be home tonight until very late," Oregon said casually.

The man had a date. That decided it. "Wait a minute, Aunt Mattie."

Green-gold eyes looked at her with an intensity that stopped breath, lungs, and heart. She blinked, gasped, and recovered enough to look outside at the sheets of rain striking the west kitchen windows. "I like to listen to the radio." She flicked a glance at Oregon.

A smile spread across his face, a satisfied, smug smile that almost made her refuse. Almost, but not quite. "We'll come if we don't have electricity. And if the rain lets up enough to get Aunt Mattie over."

"It will," he said with no room for doubt.

She had a feeling he was right. Aunt Mattie took a sip of hot coffee, then said, "That's so nice. Charity doesn't go to bed as early as I do."

Charity sent up a silent plea. Aunt Mattie, don't talk about my going to bed. The powers that be didn't acknowledge the prayer. "She's a night owl," Aunt Mattie continued. "And up out of bed early in the morning. Just not enough sleep for a healthy young woman."

Oregon looked at her, his eyes dancing with devilment. "Bed uncomfortable? Are you too tense to sleep?"

She blushed. He knew exactly what he was doing. "No. Will this rain be good for your wheat or have we had too much lately?"

He grinned an infuriating grin. "We haven't had enough rain. It'll be good for the wheat. Should be good for sleeping too. It'll be cool. I always like to sleep in the . . ." Charity held her breath with his pause, letting it out when he said, ". . . rain."

"Oh, my, yes," Aunt Mattie said. "I'll have to get out the blankets tonight."

"No, you won't, Mattie. You'll be at my house"— Oregon looked at Charity—"in my beds. I'll get out the blankets. Maybe you just need change, Charity. Maybe in my bed you won't have insomnia."

Charity fumed, looking down at her sandwich. Odious Oregon Brown fit. She wanted to tell him they wouldn't come, but she wasn't about to give up hearing Rory Runyon. Thank goodness Oregon would be out! Momentarily she wondered who dated him. What kind of woman would put up with him? Maybe he won her over with his spectacular kisses—

Someone might just as well have dumped ice water on her. Startled, she looked up to find him watching her curiously. She dropped her gaze, feeling confused. Why had she thought his kisses were spectacular?

"Charity." Aunt Mattie's voice sounded persistent.

"Yes?"

"Oregon asked if you like eggs or pancakes better?"

"Sorry, I didn't hear you." She hated his pesky smile. "Eggs. Pancakes are fattening."

His green eyes assessed her. "That shouldn't worry you, Charity."

"Thank you."

He grinned.

They ate in silence for a few minutes, then Aunt Mattie said, "Charity, we got a letter from Ziza this morning." She glanced at Oregon. "I've told you about Ziza"—Charity wondered if there was anything Mattie hadn't told Oregon—"Charity's aunt on her mother's side of the family." Aunt Mattie turned back to Charity. "She sent an announcement of her wedding."

"Again! That's number eight! I didn't know she was going with anyone."

"She said it was a whirlwind romance and they married three weeks ago in Mexico City. He's an insurance salesman and they'll live in Kansas City. They're coming to see us this weekend."

"To Enid?" Charity had a sinking feeling. She had enough problems without Ziza's adding to them. Chaos seemed to follow her tall, dark-haired aunt. She glanced at Oregon and detected a thoughtful expression in his eyes.

"Her brother-in-law, Rolf, lives in Oklahoma City, so they'll meet here. Rolf's single and she wants you to meet him."

"Oh, lordy," Charity groaned, and blushed. Why, oh, why did Aunt Mattie bring it up in front of Oregon? She refused to look at him and searched desperately in her mind for another topic. Her desperation mushroomed as Aunt Mattie turned to Oregon and added, "It worries Ziza that Charity isn't married."

"You don't say."

Charity glanced at him sharply and immediately regretted it. He grinned at her and asked with great innocence, "You anxious to get married, Charity?"

"No. The idea of spending the rest of my life with some of the men I've met is too awful for words!"

His eyes had a wickedly gleeful expression. "Too awful! Do tell. What would you like in a husband?"

Would this conversation never end? She wanted to gnash her teeth and tell Oregon to go to hell. "Kindness. I'd definitely want kindness. I think I'll have some more lemonade." Her glass was three-fourths full. She rose to get the pitcher and returned to the table. "Would you care for more, Aunt Mattie?"

Aunt Mattie shook her head.

"Kindness," Oregon mused. "Well, kindness is an admirable quality."

"What's Ziza's husband's name?" Charity asked Aunt Mattie, fighting the desire to pour the lemonade on Oregon's head.

"It's Bernard Feathers," Aunt Mattie said.

"Ziza Feathers. Will they be here long?"

"She didn't say. You know Ziza."

Too well, Charity knew Ziza. She glanced at Oregon reluctantly. "Do you care for more lemonade?"

"Yes, please. So you want a kind husband. What else?"

"A silent one."

He grinned, the dimples appeared, and she almost poured the lemonade right into his lap. If she did, it would be her luck that he would stay at their house until his jeans dried. "Kind and silent," he said. "Might be a little dull, Charity."

She compressed her lips and set the pitcher on the counter, her back to Oregon while she tried to control her temper. With an effort she smiled at him as she sat down. "I prefer everything quiet and peaceful. Very quiet."

Aunt Mattie laughed and said, "Oh, Charity, that's a good one! It's always fun when you're here." She sobered and peered through her trifocals. "I don't know what I'll do when you go." Her eyes filled with tears suddenly, and Charity reached across the table to squeeze her aunt's cold fingers.

"I'm here and I'm not leaving any time soon. Now, don't you worry." Aunt Mattie smiled and Charity turned to glare at Oregon, as if to lay the blame squarely at his feet for disturbing her aunt, but she clashed with a probing, solemn look that made her lower her lashes swiftly.

Even though the conversation turned to a safe topic, Charity thought the lunch would never end, the rain wouldn't let up, and Oregon wouldn't ever leave, but he did. After he pulled on his dry shirt, leaving it open, he handed the towel to Charity. It was warm from his body heat. She dropped in onto a chair as if it were on fire and followed him to the kitchen door. "I'll go through the back," he said.

They stood on the patio a moment. Water dripped off the roof and trees, an orchestra of plops splashing on the concrete, into puddles, and on the grass. Across the western sky a rainbow arced bright colors against an expanse of gray-blue. Charity found the golden furred chest beside her more intriguing than the sweeping colors in the sky, though.

"See you tonight," he said. "Call me and I'll come get you so your aunt won't get wet."

"Thanks, I can drive."

"Okay." He strode across the wet grass, sprang easily to the top of the fence, then dropped out of sight on the other side.

Charity spent the rest of the day alternately puttering in the garage, cleaning and sorting through things, and calling the electric company. When she finally connected, a man said lightning had knocked out lines all over Enid and it might be twenty-four hours before they could get to her neighborhood.

Disgruntled, she replaced the receiver. That meant a night at Oregon Brown's. He would be away, so it shouldn't be too disastrous. She returned to cleaning and tried not to think about the coming night.

Later she and Aunt Mattie ate another cold meal, then Charity bathed, packed a few things, gathered them up along with Aunt Mattie's, and drove around the block to Oregon Brown's.

He greeted them at the door. Tight wheat-colored jeans molded his legs, and a cream-colored knit shirt covered his chest, its color flattering to his ruddy complexion and golden hair. His tan leather boots made him tower over her more than ever. He looked appealing, very much so. If she hadn't known about his personality, she would have been quite impressed. Her heart was impressed anyway and beat double time when she passed him to enter the house.

It was a surprisingly nice house. She had expected clutter and something goatlike. Instead there were high ceilings and dark mahogany woodwork, deep beige carpeting, and comfortable, obviously expensive cherry-wood furniture.

"I'll show you your bedrooms," Oregon said cheerfully. He tucked the two small suitcases under one arm and took Aunt Mattie's arm with his other hand, leaving Charity to trail behind.

"Mattie, I gave you the downstairs bedroom, my room, so you won't have to climb the stairs."

Charity almost missed her step. She glared at Oregon's thick red-gold curls. So he would sleep upstairs with her! Getting to hear Rory Runyon was going to cost her some peace of mind.

"Would you like something to eat?" Oregon asked.

Aunt Mattie laughed. "Oh, dear me, no! We just ate. And it's my bedtime. Just let me put these old bones down to rest."

"Sure. Here we are." He led Aunt Mattie into a room while Charity stood in the doorway. It was his room, all right. Aunt Mattie would get lost in the king-sized bed that was covered by a quilted emerald-colored spread. Two brown leather wing chairs were in front of a stone fireplace. A large brown desk held neat stacks of papers and a telephone. A television was in one corner, plants lined the windows, bookshelves covered one wall.

With a vague, uneasy feeling, Charity wondered if they had prevented Oregon from bringing his date home tonight. That was neither here nor there; she shrugged the thought away. Oregon took her arm. "Mattie, Charity will come down and help you in a minute. Let me show her where she'll sleep before I go."

"Run along, dears. I can manage."

Dears. Charity was acutely aware of his fingers fastened lightly around her upper arm. They left Aunt Mattie, and Charity felt as if she had been flung to the lions. A fresh, male scent invaded her senses with subtle insistence, an odor of summer clover, of the outdoors. As they climbed the steps side by side, she longed to tell him to remove his fingers from her arm, but she didn't want to make an issue of it.

"Today," she said, "our attorneys talked about your offer for Uncle Hubert's newspaper." She slanted a look at him. "You haven't mentioned it."

"I'm interested. There's no hurry and I didn't want to rush you or Mattie. I told Jack to wait until next week to call."

She mulled over his answer. It seemed typical of his laid-back style, and she was relieved that he wouldn't pressure her for an answer. They had reached the upper hallway, which had four doors opening off it. He led the way to the farthest door on the right. She hoped his would be the farthest door on the left.

"Here we are." He opened the door and waited. To her relief his fingers dropped away from her arm. She entered a spacious bedroom with antique mahogany furniture, a large mirrored armoire, an ornately carved dresser, and a four-poster bed. It was neat and would have been a pleasant, comfortable guest bedroom except for one thing. The bed had a flaming scarlet spread turned down over black satin sheets. Black as midnight! "Maybe Aunt Mattie should stay here," she said dryly.

"This is definitely you."

Her cheeks grew warm. "I'm not the black-satin-sheet type."

"Try them and see," he said lightly as he set her suitcase down. "There's a clock-radio by the bed. Want me to show you how to set it?"

"I brought my own."

"Like to listen to the radio?"

"Yes, but I'll keep it low. It won't disturb you."

"Oh, don't worry about that. Listen all you want. What kind of music do you like?"

She didn't like his persistent questions, but she remembered Oregon was Rory's boss. She would put in a plug for Rory.

"My favorite program is one on your station."

"Do tell!"

His green eyes were beginning to look mischievous again. Well, give Rory a compliment and drop it. No doubt Oregon took credit for everything that came from his station. "Yes. I like 'Nighttime,' with Rory Runyon."

"Ahhh, you like Runyon's style."

"Yes." So there, Mr. Oregon Brown! Take a lesson. His eyes narrowed. "You like the music or Rory

Runyon?" he asked in a matter-of-fact voice, as if he were conducting a poll. No harm in telling him.

"I like Rory Runyon." She waited two heartbeats to see if he would try to make something of that. When he didn't she warmed to her subject. "He's a marvelous DJ."

"Thank you. Why do you think so?"

"Hmmm. His voice, his manner . . ." She paused again, but Oregon merely gazed back blandly. "He's so . . . so . . ."

"Sexy?" he suggested softly.

She blushed and snapped her mouth shut. She should have known better!

"There's nothing wrong with sexy," he said. "Why the blush, Charity?" His finger sailed over her cheek, leaving a trail of silvery tingles fluttering in its wake.

"Sex is personal," she muttered angrily. "I don't care to discuss sex with you."

"I can't think of a more interesting subject to discuss with you."

She shot him a dark look and saw the laughter in his eyes. "You can be so damned aggravating. I feel like packing and going home!"

He waved his arm at the door. "I'm not holding you here."

She glared at him. Once more she had to choose between Rory Runyon and Oregon Brown. Put up with one to have the other.

"You won't get to hear Rory Runyon if you go," he said.

"I'll stay. In spite of circumstances," she said with as much ice as possible. It was difficult to project ice when you were five three, had delinquent blond curls that would never behave, and big blue eyes that belonged on a doll, but she gave it a try. And while she was busy trying to be icy, Oregon moved closer.

"You know, Charity," he said, his voice thoughtful, "you really do need to be kissed."

"I—"

Someday she would learn. Too late now, for his mouth was over her open one. His long arms, steel bands, fitted her to his broad chest, against a heart that thudded while his tongue took control and ended her arguments, stirred a response, and took her breath away. Completely. And she was most thoroughly kissed.

Her system couldn't get the message that she was aggravated with Oregon Brown, that heart and pulse and metabolism should not respond. They responded shamelessly, instantly, and totally. Her arms wound around his neck and clung. He felt so good!

His big hand drifted slowly, devastatingly, down her spine, then he pressed her soft, rounded bottom to him. His hand lingered, then changed course, moving upward, molding her curves, brushing the underside of her breast. She moaned, but the sound was muffled by Oregon's mouth.

His hard arms encircled her and he picked her up. He carried her to the bed and gently lowered her to it, then lay down beside her and pulled her into his arms. A degree of sanity returned to Charity and she pushed.

He stopped instantly. She looked up at him, into green eyes darkened by passion, eyes that were like emerald seas that coaxed her to set sail, to drift in their green-gold currents. She rolled away. "Will you stop?"

"I did a second ago." He shifted onto his back and put his hands behind his head.

"I thought you were going out."

"I am, in a minute."

His words, in his husky, sexy timbre, tripped her heart into flight. He lay so close, his big body so aroused. Charity swallowed and was surprised that her throat hurt, that her whole body ached.

He smiled and stood up, and she turned her back to him.

"What's the matter, Charity?"

"Nothing."

A kiss brushed the nape of her neck, his husky voice coming with his minty breath. "See you later."

And then he was gone. Warmth, disturbing and erotic, went with him. Relief came, and, to her surprise, disappointment. She wished he hadn't been going out. The thought shocked her. Long ago she had vowed she would never be trapped into the situation her Aunt Ziza was in—drifting from husband to husband or relationship to relationship because of loneliness or vulnerability. After having lived through one of Aunt Ziza's divorces and marriages, Charity had vowed she would never enter into a relationship lightly. If she were to commit herself seriously to a man, she wanted to know him long and well first. Oregon Brown was a definite threat to her resolution! Thoughts of Oregon sent her to her suitcase for the list of four songs she wanted to request, just to hear Rory Runyon say the words back to her again like the night before.

"I'll Have to Say I Love You in a Song," "You Are So Beautiful"—She blushed just looking at that one. No one had ever said that to her. This was her only chance—"When a Man Loves a Woman" and "Touch Me in the Morning."

She moved the last one up on the list. She just had to hear him say, "Touch me . . ."

She laid aside the list and went downstairs to see about Aunt Mattie. She was already asleep, so Charity turned out the light and closed the door, then decided to prowl through Oregon's house. The decor was amazingly lovely. There were antique cut-glass crystal pitchers and bowls filling an old-fashioned curved glass front china cabinet. The kitchen was filled with modern appliances, warm oak cabinets, and had a bright yellow floor. Oregon obviously loved color. The house was a rainbow of tasteful colors set against a pale beige carpet. The living room had a big fireplace, a Chickering grand piano, a stereo console, and comfortable furniture.

It didn't fit him. In her mind he belonged in a grass shack on a tropical island. He and Billy. She gazed out one of the kitchen windows, shivering. Thank goodness the goat wasn't a house pet!

Finally it was time for 'Nighttime' and Rory Runyon's adorable, husky voice. She put on a red-and-white polka-dot nightie, picked up her list, placed the phone beside the bed, and turned on the radio.

The black satin sheets were cool against her skin. She ran her fingers across a pillow slip. Why did Oregon have black satin sheets? She didn't want to speculate on that one! But for a fleeting moment she remembered lying in his arms. It had felt good. She closed her eyes and thought about Oregon's embrace, his kiss, and Rory Runyon.

She made a mental note to brave the teasing and ask Oregon for a picture of Rory Runyon. Then Rory's husky voice glided into the room, circling, floating to caress her waiting nerves, to take her breath away.

"Hi, darlin'. I couldn't wait to be with you. We're going to listen to some music. Just you and me, darlin'. Let's do this together."

A song began and Charity gulped and blinked in the darkness, remembering Oregon's hot kiss. Her body was aching. She wanted to be kissed, to be touched. She rolled over and peered at the radio. A brown radio. She tried to envision Tom Selleck with black hair, but all she could see were green-gold eyes and freckles.

She sat up. Oregon Brown was interfering with Rory Runyon. The damned green eyes and curly golden-red hair and freckles interfered, along with broad shoulders and muscles and deviltry!

She gritted her teeth and wriggled her hips in a determined effort to get Oregon Brown firmly out of her mind. If only she could think about Oregon's kiss and see Rory's face, just fantasize and have the perfect—She blinked. The perfect male? Oregon's kisses were that good?

The record ended and Rory came on, his voice taking away her bad images, her worrisome thoughts. She sank down in bed, soothed by velvety, smooth tones that caressed her in the dark. And he finally came to what she had been waiting for. His voice drifted over her senses as he said, "Darlin', call me."

She did with such haste, she almost dropped the phone. Then his voice reached her through the line.

"Rory, this is Charity."

"Charity, darlin'." She melted. "I've been waitin' for you to call me," he whispered. "I was afraid you wouldn't. What song would you like to hear, darlin'?"

She swallowed. Her palms were damp and a blush scorched her cheeks. Thank goodness for darkness, for anonymity!

"Will you play 'I'll Have to Say I Love You in a Song'?"

"Darlin', of course. I'd like to hold you in my arms, Charity, while I play this."

Charity thought she would faint. His marvelous voice, the seductive words, made her ache as her hips moved slightly. His voice didn't ease her longing; it stirred it to monumental proportions.

She closed her eyes and clutched the phone while hot, golden words flowed over her, burning as they went down, starting a fire in her lower regions.

"Would you like to be in my arms, darlin'?"

"Yes . . ." Lord, yes!

"I want to hold you next to my heart. Settle your head back into my shoulder. Here, darlin'. Here's 'I'll Have to Say . . . I Love You . . . in a Song.' "

The pauses almost finished her off. "I Love You," said in his fluid, amber voice, made her groan in the darkness.

"Charity . . ."

"Yes, Rory?" She waited breathlessly.

"I'm glad you called. I really have been waiting."

He sounded as if he meant it. She wondered how many women he told that to, but didn't really care. It sounded so good!

"My blond Charity. I'd like to hold you for this song. Can you imagine my arms around you?"

She couldn't answer. She tried to breathe and finally whispered, "Yes." She remembered strong arms, a warm, male body, and tried to forget the face that went with it.

"Can you imagine my lips on yours?"

Shocked at his boldness, she looked at the phone. Lord, the man was coming on strong! Since when did disc jockeys get so personal? "Is this going to be an obscene phone call? You're sure we're not on the air?"

He chuckled and she wilted. Each little baritone sound carried a seductive tickle. "We're not on the air, darlin'. The 'I Love You' song is."

Her heart might not survive the song.

"Charity, can you imagine my kiss? I'd like to kiss you, darlin'."

Her eyes widened and she stared at the receiver again. He might get himself in trouble if he said that to every woman who called KKZF. "Do you say that to everyone?"

"This is a first."

A first! Something soft wrapped around her heart and squeezed lightly.

"Charity, I mean it. I'd like to kiss you, darlin'."

"I'd like you to." Dreamily, she added, "And that's a first."

"First time you've wanted—"

"First time I've told a man I wanted his kiss," she interrupted him hastily.

"We'll have a lot of firsts, Charity. I'd like to touch your soft cheeks, your silky hair, to hold you, to talk to you, to kiss you and caress you. . . ."

Charity shifted in bed, squeezed her eyes shut, moistened her lips unconsciously. This radio business wasn't good for her constitution. Rory Craig Runyon's voice was a health hazard. She wanted to ask him why he had singled her out so swiftly from his other callers, but she was afraid. And she didn't really believe that she was the only one.

"Charity, the song's going to end. Will you call me back tonight?"

"Yes," she whispered.

"You have another song to request?"

"As a matter of fact, I do."

"Good, darlin'. That's my girl. Here we go on the air."

The music ended and he asked, "How's that, darlin'? Did you like your song?"

"I loved it," she gasped.

" 'I'll Have to Say I Love You in a Song.' What a nice way to say it. This is a good night for a song like that. It's nice outside, a beautiful May evening, about sixty-five degrees, stars out, not a cloud in sight. Wasn't that a storm we had today? Now the clouds are gone and it's a perfect night to hold you close and listen to music. Call me again, Charity. 'Nii-aight, darlin'."

" 'Night, Rory." Charity collapsed on the pillow, clinging to the phone. She longed to be held. She ground her teeth and groaned. A big golden body was damned difficult to forget.

She spent the next two hours, all of Rory Runyon's 'Nighttime,' alternately agonizing and delighting in his voice. She called twice more. The second time she lost her courage and couldn't ask for "You Are So Beautiful." It might be too obvious. Rory Runyon was sexy, and he might also be smart. So she requested "When a Man Loves a Woman."

" 'When a Man Loves a Woman,' " he repeated, after putting on the record and telling her their conversation wasn't on the air. "Charity, want to know how I'd love a woman?"

The man was oversexed. "Yes," she whispered, trembling, blushing in the dark bedroom. She wanted to hear, but she didn't want to. She hoped he wouldn't get obscene. She couldn't hang up on Rory Runyon. She held her breath as he whispered throatily, his voice coming up as if from the molten center of the earth, slowly rising to air, "I'd hold you next to my heart, Charity."

She let out her breath. Nothing scandalous so far. Just delightful, so sexy! "I'd kiss you all night long, kiss you so slowly, darlin'. Charity, are you there?"

It took a second, but she found her voice and answered, "Yes."

"Good. I'd kiss you so slowly, all over, every beautiful, adorable inch of you, your throat, your lips, your . . . sweet shoulders. I'd run my fingers through your hair and hold you close. I want to touch you, Charity. . . ."

Aflame with his words, Charity closed her eyes as his husky, sensuous voice seemed to caress her body. In spite of their nebulous airiness, his words had a blazing effect. Breathing heavily, she clutched the phone. Hunger uncoiled, expanding with heat to permeate her veins and bones. She writhed and groaned.

"What's that, darlin? Did you say something?"

Her eyes flew open. "Oh!"

"I thought you said something to me, Charity."

Silence. She couldn't say a word. She shook and knotted the sheet in her fist. He chuckled softly. "Darlin', the song's almost over. We'll be back on the air. Call me again. Can you stay awake until the last of the show?"

She almost laughed at the ridiculousness of his question. "Yes."

"Call me during the last thirty minutes of the show, darlin'."

"I will."

And she did. She clutched the phone, burned with embarrassment, but bravely requested "Touch Me in the Morning."

" 'Touch Me in the Morning,' " he repeated, and she dissolved into jelly.

The words made her want to touch him . . . and the only man she could think of was Oregon Brown! She clenched her hands and fought to mentally see Tom Selleck instead.

"So here we are in the early hours of the mornin' and we have a request for 'Touch Me in the Morning,' " Rory said. "Beautiful. It's late. Lay your head on the pillow, darlin', close your eyes, and think of me."

The music commenced. Charity's heart pranced like a racehorse at the starting gate. The voice she waited to hear came on, speaking softly to her alone.

"Darlin', I like your request. I really like that title." His voice deepened to a purring rumble. "Darlin', are you in bed?"

She couldn't answer this time. She listened in silence to the song.

"Charity, are you there?"

"Hmmmm."

He chuckled. "What's the matter, darlin'?"

"Hmmmm."

He sighed, a tremulous breath that rasped through the line into her nervous system. How could a soft, tiny noise trigger destruction?

"Ahh, Charity, you must be sleepy, darlin'. Drowsy. I wish I could hold your sweet body next to mine."

How did he get away with indiscriminately saying things like that to women he didn't know? How did he know whether his listeners had a boyfriend or an irate husband who might walk in on the conversation? Charity wondered about it fleetingly, then tossed her curiosity aside. Who cared? She loved

every word! She would miss Enid when she had to g
home to Tulsa.

"Charity . . ."

She opened her eyes. Surely her mouth, throat
windpipe, brain could function enough to get out on
word. "Yes?"

"I'm so glad you called me. I can just picture you i
my arms, darlin'. I want to hold you, love. Hold you
and kiss you until you melt."

She did melt, into a puddle of volatile desire tha
hovered on the brink of spontaneous combustion.

"It's late, darlin'. I'm going to sign off soon, g
home to bed."

She shook. No one had ever crammed so much sex
feeling into a one-syllable word. *B-e-d*. Only, said b
Rory Runyon, it was a two-syllable word. Oh, my
Maybe she shouldn't listen to him for a few nights.

"Darlin', I have to sign off. Think about me, Char
ity. I'll think about you, about 'Touch Me in the Morn
ing.' 'Night, darlin'."

"Hmmmm."

She hung up the phone, but she couldn't hang u
herself. Her nerves had spun into tangled string
Knotted was more like it. She stared into the dark
ness, miserable, aching, and more lonely than ever
After enough flounces to twist the sheet into a rope
she sat up, turned on the bedside lamp, and looked
for something to read. There was a book on the bot
tom shelf of the small chest beside the bed.

History of Railways in Mexico. Maybe Mexican
railroads would be an antidote for Rory Runyon. She
opened the book and began to read. Her eyes followed
each line obediently, but her brain and her body were
over a thousand miles north of Mexican railways.

A light rap on the door made her raise her head.

Five

Surprised, her thoughts on other things, she answered without hesitation. "Come in."

Oregon did. He paused in the doorway, big and sexy in his tight jeans, his lashes drooping over his eyes. In his hands he held two mugs. He kicked the door shut and walked toward her. "I saw your light and thought we'd have a nightcap."

Her brain finally began to function, to stir out of the euphoria caused by Rory. Little bells began to tinkle a warning, then, as Oregon approached the bed, they started to toll like the bells of Notre Dame.

"Oregon, it's a little late." Oh, lord, she sounded so breathless!

"I know. That's why I thought you'd enjoy a nightcap." He sat down beside her and held out a mug.

She expected hot chocolate, or maybe plain milk,

but instead there was a bubbly, pale yellow liquid in the mug. "What's this?"

"Champagne. Here's to a bolt of lightning." He held out his mug.

She tried to gather her wits, along with her caution and reserve. "Listen, I can't—"

He placed his finger on her lips. "Shh. Raise your mug, Charity." He smiled. His green-gold eyes looked as inviting as a spring meadow filled with buttercups. One of his knees was pressing lightly against her thigh. He smelled so good, as he always did, and his invitation sounded harmless. She raised her mug and tapped his. He drank, his eyes never leaving hers, watching her over the rim of his white mug. The gaze was too intense, and looking into his eyes was like staring at the sun. She twiddled with the covers and sipped the bubbly champagne. Oregon set his mug on the bedside chest and reached down to tug off his boots.

"What're you doing?" She gazed at him in horror.

He smiled. Another charming, quiet smile. "My feet hurt. Do you mind?"

"No." But she knew there was a catch in it somewhere. He was up to no good. Just as sure as she drew breath, the man had evil intentions. Maybe not evil, just . . . wicked. Why was he sitting beside her at almost three in the morning, taking off his boots after being out all evening? There were a few answers, and she didn't like any of them. Maybe he had been turned down and wanted to ease his frustration. Well, that had to be straightened out quickly. "Did you just take your date home?"

His eyes began to twinkle. "No. I work at night."

"Oh! You work?"

He grinned. "Thought I was a lazy, good-for-nothing, didn't you?"

"Well, when you find a man in a hammock in the middle of the morning . . ."

". . . you ought to stretch out with him."

She laughed. She'd walked right into that one. So he had been at work. "Where do you work?" She didn't feel inclined to mention the paper, and evidently he didn't either.

"At KKZF. I go down at night, when it's quieter. I can take care of necessary business. I don't go every night." He picked up the book she'd been reading. "You're interested in railroads too? Isn't that a remarkable coincidence!"

He sounded so happy that she had to admit the truth. "No, I found it beside the bed. I couldn't sleep."

"Oh, yeah, your sleep problem. You need to relax, Charity. That's why I brought the champagne." His voice was a low rumble. While he talked, he unfastened the second button of his shirt, revealing the red-gold curls that gave his body a golden glow.

"What're you doing? Don't tell me your chest hurts!"

He smiled, a lazy smile, coaxing her to relax. "I'm hot."

She was, too. She drank faster. If she finished off the champagne, he would go.

His big fingers undid another button. She stared as if drawn by a magnet. The curls covered a magnificent expanse of muscles and burnished skin. His voice lowered a fraction, reminding her of Rory Runyon's. "What did you do tonight?"

She blushed. She bent her head and wished she had long hair that would tumble forward and hide her face. He lifted her chin with his fingers. "Charity, you're blushing!" He looked both amused and satisfied. "What have you been up to?" He laughed softly. "Maybe I shouldn't ask."

"I've been listening to the radio!" she snapped, and flounced down onto the pillow, thereby committing two tactical mistakes at once.

He leaned over, placing his arms on either side of her, to pin her down. "You've been listening to 'Nighttime.' " It was a statement, not a question. It didn't matter, she couldn't have answered anyway. Oregon was so close, his marvelous mouth only a foot above her, his sweet scent teasing her, his green eyes promising excitement, his muscled arms so inviting. The golden froth of hair on his broad chest made her want to reach up and touch him. He trailed his fingers along her shoulder, as lightly as a wind song. The whispering stroke worked its own magic chemistry, changing his touch to shimmering tingles that twisted and spun through her veins.

His head lowered, his mouth met hers.

She turned her head. "Oregon, don't, please. I barely know you . . ."

"But there's a special chemistry between us," he whispered, and placed his lips firmly on hers, opening hers with an expertise that allowed no resistance. She closed her eyes and her head started spinning. One mug of champagne, Oregon's kiss, Rory's voice, and she was duck soup. In fairness she acknowledged that it was a big mug, Runyon's voice had had her quivering with readiness, and Oregon's kiss was definitely spectacular!

She squeezed her eyes shut tightly until she was whirling amid flaming reds, blues, greens, flecked with gold. Their champagne breaths mingled as their tongues danced to a silent melody.

Oregon's big hand trailed over her shoulder and down, bulldozing the polka-dot cotton out of his way. His touch was like warm sunshine as he laid his hand over her breast. Streams of sweet agony pulsed from the peak that firmed against his palm. Charity shifted, and the movement was startlingly erotic. She moaned, but his mouth caught the sound and drowned it.

Somewhere in her there should be a protest, but she couldn't locate it. She hadn't had that much champagne, but she'd been too lonely, too aroused. Her body was clamoring for more of Oregon—and he was marvelous! His kiss continued relentlessly, a sweet, throbbing agony that made her shift closer to him. She wanted him. As judgment went down, her arms went up. The fingers of one hand slipped into his luxuriant red-gold curls while her other hand trailed over his powerful shoulders.

"Touch me, Charity . . ."

Her eyes flew open. He sounded like Rory. Suddenly she wondered if he had listened to Rory's program. He would've heard Rory say her name, heard her requests. She twisted her head. "Did you listen to 'Nighttime'?"

His thick golden-brown lashes lifted slowly and his green eyes seemed to envelop her. "Sure. I heard your request, 'Touch Me . . .' And I will."

He knew! But her anger was banked before it flared into existence. His mouth returned to possess hers, to gather her moist warmth, her thoughts, her reason, and her objections, dissolving all.

Her fingers explored his solid muscles, sliding down his smooth back to his narrow waist. He felt so good to her, so right against her. Her thoughts swirled and ran together like spilled wine. Where was her long, firm resolve not to get involved with a man until she knew him well? Was she vulnerable because of loneliness or did she want Oregon that badly? Logical answers were impossible; her questions were tossed away in a tempest caused by his strong hands.

His lips trailed over her cheek, down her throat, leaving fire dancing on her skin. Oregon was slow, deliberate, so careful. His touch was gentle, arousing her with the faintest strokes, making her writhe in his arms and cling to his narrow waist. He stroked her breasts, his breath drifting over the eager nipples. She craved more until finally his tongue flicked a rosy peak. She moaned softly, twisting to thrust her hips against his hard body.

His hands were everywhere, touching her with long, slow strokes, with short, deft brushes. She wound her fingers in his hair, letting the thick, soft curls tickle her palms until he pulled away to shed his clothes. Through lowered lashes she looked at a body that was a work of art. Amber flesh dusted with freckles, broad shoulders, the narrow hips and flat, hard stomach . . . all were poetry, a song of male virility. Her gaze drifted down, and a blush seared her. He was so totally male, so big and gorgeous! He lowered himself beside her and slipped the nightie with its elasticized top down over her hips and legs, his lips following its course.

Her eyes closed as she clung to him, and she gasped as his tongue tasted her sweet flesh. No man had ever made love to her like this. Never had her body become an object of joy, of wonder. Plundering kisses drove her to abandon. She relinquished logic and cared only about Oregon. Each kiss, each stroke by his big fingers broke a link in the chain of her resistance. With his hands exploring her body, his mouth raining hot, devastating kisses, his husky voice whispering tantalizing words, he drove her to a quivering, gasping brink. His big hands molded her soft curves, heightening her need into a frenzy, until finally he parted her thighs and carefully lowered himself to her.

She clung to him wildly, arching her hips with desperate urgency. The first thrust caused a sharp stab of pain as his hard body invaded her softness, tearing into her. Her eyes flew open as she tried not to cry out.

His own eyes opened wide in shock. She realized that her status had never occurred to him. He started to withdraw, but she tightened her arms and her knees.

"Oregon," she whispered. Her hips twisted and he was beyond the point of return.

He moved slowly, carefully, his lips raining kisses on her shoulder, her throat, her mouth. Pain slowly changed, easing, transforming into sheer pleasure. When the shuddering climax came, she cried out softly while she clung to him, both frightened and exhilarated by the intense sensations. He caught her cry with his mouth, kissing her deeply as he continued to move, until he stiffened and moaned deep in his throat. She held on to him tightly as his body relaxed and lay heavily on her.

She felt complete with Oregon, floating on a silky sea of bliss. He shifted beside her, pulling her to him, fitting her head onto his shoulder, her leg over his, her soft breasts against his chest and side. He kissed her forehead and stroked her cheek, and when he spoke his voice was husky yet gentle, like spring mist.

"Ahh, Charity, darlin'."

Charity's eyes opened wide. She looked up at his firm, freckled jaw, golden lashes on a freckled cheek. No one else could say "Charity, darlin'," that same way. Oregon Brown was Rory Runyon!

Six

His lips trailed over her cheek, her temple, down to nibble her earlobe, then lower to her shoulder. "Charity, darlin', I didn't know. Why didn't you tell me?"

She barely heard the question, gave it no conscious consideration as she mulled over her discovery. Oregon Brown was Rory Runyon! Her thoughts were as busy with the revelation as ants that had discovered a lump of sugar.

Oregon propped himself up on an elbow and looked at her solemnly, brushing her tangled curls away from her face. As she gazed back at his thoughtful green eyes, his furrowed brow, she thought about Rory's deep, golden voice.

"Why didn't you tell me?" Oregon asked. "I thought . . ."

It was him, all right. Why hadn't she realized sooner? There was a difference in resonance, probably because of the microphone. Why hadn't he told her?

"Darlin', Did I hurt you badly?"

He had known all along. All the calls, the questions. *Want to know how I'd love a woman?* Like a boulder toppling off a cliff, her thoughts came roaring down, furiously gaining momentum.

"Oh, darlin'. If you'd only told me. Charity, I don't know what to say. . . ."

He had set her up with his sensuous voice, he had made love to her over the phone and over the radio! Oregon and Rory! She felt dazed. Rory Runyon didn't tell all his callers how he'd like to make love to them! He had told her to drive her to a quivering, melting readiness!

"Oh, love, you're so quiet. Charity, say something to me. This is the first time this has happened to me. Please say something."

Well, it sure as hell was the first time it had happened to her! After all her years of caution, she had succumbed swiftly to a husky voice and seductive kisses! Rory Runyon, Oregon Brown! And even now he hadn't admitted the truth. All he had done was say, "Yes, I listened to 'Nighttime.' "

"Oh, Charity, you don't know what you're doing to me, darlin'." He lay back down and fitted her to his side, putting his arms around her while he gazed up at the ceiling. She lay against him, her head on his shoulder, her stomach pressing his hard hipbone, their legs touching, while her thoughts churned madly. She had been seduced by Rory Runyon! A tingle of sheer delight danced in her veins. And it had been so good—as good as his voice had hinted it would be!

"Darlin', it was good. . . ."

She blinked, finally settling her attention on Oregon. She recalled the words that had drifted through a nebulous layer of consciousness in the past few minutes. *Why didn't you tell me? . . . I don't know what to say. . . . it was good . . . if you'd only told me . . .*

If she had told him she was a virgin, would he have not seduced her? What was Oregon hinting at, regret? And still he didn't say, "Darlin', I have a confession. I'm Rory."

Her mind gnawed over the facts, grinding down one after another. And another whisper returned to haunt her. With the first kiss, Oregon had said, "There's a special chemistry between us." Was it special to him? She wasn't sure what she felt for Oregon, and she wanted to be very sure before she let herself get tangled up with a man.

"Charity, I wish you'd say something! Don't be angry, darlin'."

Angry? She was on a roller coaster between anger and ecstasy. She had been loved, kissed, and caressed by Rory Runyon, by Oregon Brown. Ecstasy, joy, rapture. Then down she went, with the aggravating knowledge that he had tricked her and still hadn't admitted the truth.

She mulled it over. She wouldn't tell Oregon that she knew he was Rory. She would wait and see when the truth crossed his lips. His lips. She sighed in contentment.

"Oh, Charity . . ." He shifted and gazed down at her, his thick brows drawn together, his forehead creased in a frown. Solemnly she looked up at him.

"Darlin', it was wonderful. Say something. Don't be angry over something so good."

She reached up and twisted a soft red-gold curl

around her finger. She wanted to hold him, to say she knew; she wanted to cry out, "Why didn't you tell me the truth?"

Finally she said, "It was good, Oregon."

His gaze bore into her as if attempting to discern her soul. His big hand lightly stroked her shoulder as if he needed to reassure himself she was still in his arms.

"Do you hurt?"

She shook her head, and he smiled. Joy burst inside her at the expression on his face. He looked so delighted in her, so happy! And she felt the same toward him—except, why hadn't he told her the truth? *Men.* But then, how could she expect to understand a man who kept a goat for a lawn mower?

He leaned down and kissed her ear, his moist tongue touching lightly as he whispered, "Next time, darlin', it'll be better."

Next time. The words started a blaze. Next time and next time and next time. Was she falling in love with Oregon/Rory? He settled down beside her and pulled her closer, a blissful sigh escaping his lips. " 'Night, Charity."

" 'Night, Oregon." She closed her eyes, shoving all the dilemmas into a compartment of her brain and closing it down for the night. Tomorrow she would worry about Oregon/Rory, about Aunt Mattie, about Ziza's visit and the man she wanted Charity to meet, about money and the thousand other little details that required her attention. Right now she wanted to relish Oregon's big, strong arms around her, his good, male scent, listen to his heart beat beneath her bare flesh and remember the past hour. *Charity, darlin'* . . . oooh! The mere thought made her heart jump. She had been loved by Rory Runyon! Ecstasy!

Vaguely she wondered why she had been so controlled with men in her life before, men she had dated for months and resisted without heartbreak, and then had melted for Oregon like whipped cream on burning charcoals.

Yet how could she resist? There was a spark with Oregon. Maybe too much of one sometimes, but a definite spark. His kisses were fantastic! And he was Rory Runyon. Perfection. Oregon's big body, his good-natured humor, his easygoing manner, and Rory's voice. Her sigh of contentment was a whisper in the dark. Tomorrow she would look at the problems and worry about rushing into involvement with Oregon.

Drifting on a cloud in a cotton-wrapped world of gray, Charity's first conscious awareness was of a whispered caress, a touch on her thigh. She stirred slightly, too sleep-filled to wake fully and open her eyes. The enticing tingle continued. Light, feathery touches brushed over breast and hip, across her flat stomach. She moved her hips and stretched, content, dreaming of Oregon now. Warm breath wafted over her throat, her ear. A moist tongue-tip touched her ear, and her eyes finally opened.

The room was dim, silent, and dusky with the first faint streaks of dawn. She was lying in Oregon's arms, facing him, pressed to his broad chest while he stroked and kissed her awake.

" 'Morning', darlin'," he murmured, and her temperature rose. She forgot what he had just said. Suddenly it was imperative to hold him, to touch him. She wanted his warmth, his big solid body, his magic words. She wound her arms around his neck and smiled.

" 'Morning, Oregon."

A fire blazed in his green eyes, erasing the rest of the world. "This time will be better, darlin'," he whispered before he kissed her.

Better? Better than ecstasy? The magic sparks that his kiss set off ignited her entire body, and for the next hour it never occurred to her to protest. Oregon kissed her fervently while his caresses set her aflame with longing. His big hands roamed down the sweet curve of her spine, molding her to him while his lips at her throat and ear and nape built intense desire. He shifted to kiss her breasts, the soft, full contours and the rosy, wanton peaks. He was more leisurely this time as he exlored her body, discovering what aroused her until finally he possessed her completely.

He thrust into her softness, driving her to an urgency, a turbulent craving that she hadn't known was possible. She clung to him with abandon as they reached the brink, then crashed over, drifting down in a golden world of rapture.

While his weight pressed her into the bed, Oregon murmured endearments in his husky, amber voice, words that made her feel as if she belonged in his arms forever.

He rolled onto his back, pulling her to him, and together they watched the sun's glowing rays spill silently into the room, splashing across the bed, lending a rosy hue to their replete bodies.

But finally she had to face reality, had to step out of the fantastic dreamworld Oregon had created. She sat up. "Oregon, I have to get breakfast and take Aunt Mattie home."

"Lie down, darlin'. I'll cook breakfast and then take Mattie home."

"I can't stay up here in your bed! Aunt Mattie would go into shock."

He chuckled as he pulled her back down. "No, she wouldn't. I won't be here with you—not while I cook and take her home."

She pushed away from him and slid off the bed. "I can't stay in bed all day!"

He put his hands behind his head as his eyes devoured her naked body languorously. His relentless gaze sparked her modesty. Blushing, she snatched up the black satin sheet and wrapped it around her.

"Stop that, Oregon! And cover yourself, please!"

"Don't be a spoilsport, Charity. Black satin is pretty sexy on you."

"Oregon, stop! These sheets are scandalous!" And his marvelous reddish-gold body was overpowering as it lay stretched out on one.

He raised a brow. "Want to make them more scandalous?"

"No! You're oversexed!"

He shook his head, grinning crookedly, as he stood up. "No, I'm entranced, beguiled, by a gorgeous, luscious pair of . . . blue eyes."

"Oregon Brown! Stop this minute!" She thought she was going to melt, just like the Wicked Witch of the West. With a mighty effort she summoned her wits and her sternest voice, and said, "I can't lie around all day in a bed or a hammock. I have things to do."

"Oh, my, aren't we fierce this morning!" He started around the bed to her, and her heart began pounding wildly.

"Oregon . . ."

He wrapped his arms around her. "Mmmm, you smell so nice. Sweet Charity."

"I have to get dressed and go home." She sounded as firm as water. He smiled, and it took the wind out of her sails. She raised her chin and hoped that he wouldn't notice her resolve was fading. "Oregon."

"Okay, darlin'. I'm gone."

He picked up his clothes and left, leaving her in a daze. What had happened to her life? It had changed so swiftly. She couldn't imagine a time when she hadn't known Oregon. Her flesh still felt the lingering brush of his fingers. The bed was rumpled from his weight, from his marvelous big body. The sheet wrapped around her had a faint trace of his clean masculine scent. And at the moment it was impossible to summon regret for her actions.

After she had bathed and dressed, she made the bed, looking for the last time at the black satin sheets and seeing Oregon's golden body stretched out on them. Had he planned the seduction when he had made the bed up with black sheets? Was that a habit he had? She ground her teeth as she went downstairs to have breakfast with Oregon and Aunt Mattie.

Oregon, looking so appealing in his faded jeans and pale blue knit shirt, had eggs, toast, bacon, and hot coffee ready. As she watched him move around the kitchen, a thousand questions ran through her mind. She felt befuddled, as if she were caught by a force she couldn't battle, a surging sea that whirled her along on giddy currents. Every look he gave her seemed to hold its own special meaning, a confirmation of something unique and wonderful they had discovered in each other. And he couldn't stop smiling at her, showing off his dimples and making her smile right back at him, until she wondered why Aunt Mattie didn't notice the charged atmosphere.

After breakfast Charity drove downtown to talk to Mr. Wurley, the editor of the newspaper. An hour later, when she stepped outside, the hot May sunshine poured over her, shimmering on the sidewalk, making it sparkle. Across the street the courthouse on the square was shaded by tall trees. On the blocks surrounding it, people strolled in and out of shops and offices. She turned, her gaze resting briefly on the glass front of the newspaper office. She knew nothing about journalism and she had a buyer. Both she and Mr. Wurley agreed, the best thing to do would be to sell the paper to Oregon. She suspected Mr. Wurley was relieved about the decision, he knew and liked Oregon. She headed for the car to phone her attorney about her decision. An audit had already commenced, and she would need an appraisal. The paper was solvent, and from what Mr. Oppenheim, her attorney, had said, there would be enough money to set up a nice trust for Aunt Mattie.

As Charity drove home she mulled over the future. She was going to sell the paper. Now, what would she do about Aunt Mattie? The money from the sale would take care of her financially, but Mattie was too elderly to live alone, too forgetful. Charity debated giving up her own apartment and moving to Enid, or taking Aunt Mattie to Tulsa. Neither was a good idea. And even as she worried over her problems, beneath the surface of her thoughts floated an uncertain element that could affect the solutions—Oregon. Did she want to settle in Enid, find a job here, and stay close to Oregon? Would he really want her to, or had their intimacy been something casual to him? She was appalled at how little she knew about him. Yet, in ways, she felt as if she knew Oregon better than anyone else—a knowledge with a depth of quality that had nothing to do with time. Why hadn't he told her he was Rory? She remembered his laugh, his kisses, his passionate lovemaking, and a blush heated her cheeks.

Setting her jaw in a determined line, she turned around and drove back to Aunt Mattie's bank. She asked to see Mr. Simpson, the banker who had handled Uncle Hubert's affairs for years. Less than half an hour later, Charity headed home again, in more of a dilemma than ever. Mr. Simpson had politely discussed her financial situation and, to Charity's surprise, agreed to make her a loan to set her up in the landscape business in Enid if she wanted. What should she do? Stay in Enid near Mattie and Oregon and go deeper into debt, or go back to Tulsa and get a job? No easy answer had come by the time she drove up the driveway, and her thoughts had settled on Oregon. She didn't want to be like Ziza. In the past she had so carefully avoided casual relationships, then had fallen for Oregon like an uprooted tree! Well, it still wasn't too late to get to know him much better. And with that pleasant prospect in mind, she spent the rest of the afternoon helping Aunt Mattie sort through things in the garage. She was delighted when Oregon dropped by at around three, although she paid more attention to his splendid body as he moved heavy boxes and furniture for them than to her own sorting.

At five o'clock Charity asked him to stay for dinner, but he declined, saying he had to go to the station. As they stood alone in the garage, he rested his arms on her shoulders, toying with the neck of her T-shirt, stroking her throat with his fingers. She looked up into his eyes and her pulse jumped. She saw the message in those eyes, the smoldering hunger. His compelling voice was soft as he said, "I want to have you for dinner tomorrow night."

Was she in love with him—or was it merely sex? Last night had been spectacular enough to addle the most jaded mind. In her innocence, how was she to judge her emotions? She continued to stare at him, and was surprised when his brows drew together. He leaned forward and peered at her intently.

"We can just eat peanut butter sandwiches at my house if it would make it easier." He continued to study her closely. "Charity, what's on your mind?" His voice had changed suddenly, deepened, and she wondered what he had discovered in her eyes.

For just two seconds she considered blurting out the truth, that she might be in love with him. Then she remembered his deceit, his unscrupulous—was it really unscrupulous?—seduction over the airwaves with his golden, sexy voice. As she stood in indecision, one of Oregon's brows arched over his eye, giving him a devilish look. "Charity, it's just a neighborly dinner. I've already asked Mattie and she accepted for both of you."

"Why didn't you tell me!" she exclaimed angrily.

"I wanted to see what you'd say."

"You know, you have a deceitful streak in you!"

He blushed! A red flush crept up his cheeks, suffusing his face with a rosy glow. It served him right.

"My intentions are good," he said, so sincerely that she felt mollified. If he had stopped there, he would have been ahead, but he added, "Even if my actions aren't."

The teasing gleam was back in his eyes. She didn't know what she felt and she didn't have the smallest inkling about Oregon's feelings, so she kept quiet and didn't say a word.

"I've got to run, honey," he said. The look in his green eyes was inviting, and she leaned toward him a fraction of an inch. His arms went around her instantly and he kissed her. Soundly. So soundly she forgot where she was, that Aunt Mattie might walk in on them, that she didn't want to rush into an affair, that Oregon could be aggravating. She loved every second of his kiss and returned it with enthusiasm. Finally he released her slightly, raising his head to gaze into her eyes. "You have the bluest eyes I've ever seen, Charity. So big and blue I feel I could drown in them."

Each word was a drop of hot, sweet syrup running through her insides. She trembled, and her hands tightened on his hard biceps. "For someone who spends his days lying in a hammock, you have some big muscles."

He smiled, a slow lifting of the corners of his perfect mouth. "I do a few other things." He could make anything sound suggestive. Sound deliciously naughty and enticing. She wanted to wrap her arms around him and cling forever. His arms tightened a fraction. "I'm going to be late for an appointment. I have a meeting at my office in fifteen minutes."

"I'm not keeping you," she said, but her mind wasn't on what she was saying. It was concentrating on green eyes, a beautiful mouth, a strong body . . .

He leaned down for one more long kiss that left her dazed when he released her. He touched the tip of her nose with his forefinger. " 'Bye, hon. I'll miss you tonight. See you tomorrow."

" 'Bye, Oregon," she whispered. She watched him stride down the driveway, his broad shoulders swinging a fraction, golden curls ruffled by the wind, his long legs covering the distance easily, his tight jeans clinging to narrow hips and trim buttocks. And she remembered in the finest detail every inch of his golden skin. "Oh, my," she breathed softly. "Oregon Brown."

She wandered into her room, closing the door for privacy, and stared at her image in the dresser mirror. She looked as if she had been kissed. Or struck by lightning. Her lips were slightly red, swollen from Oregon's touch. She tried to raise one eyebrow the way he did. Both brows climbed. She couldn't do it. She held one brow and tried to raise the other. How did he manage that look? With both brows arched she looked in shock; he had looked so sexy. Her toes curled as she stared into the mirror and saw Oregon, one brow raised, his gaze intent and mocking, teasing her.

And then it dawned on her that if they went to dinner, he would have to tell her about Rory Runyon because he would have to go to work. Except Aunt Mattie would be with her and they would go home early. Well, she'd fix that! As she turned away to go back to work, a smile curved her rosy lips.

When the evening came, Charity felt an inner tension coiling and tightening. She couldn't wait to hear "Nighttime"! Would Oregon reveal his identity? Her nerves were raw with anticipation. She told Aunt Mattie good night, worked furiously cleaning out kitchen drawers, then bathed, taking her time, scrubbing herself, reliving every glorious second of the previous night. She dressed in a pale blue cotton nightie, then looked over the list of titles she wanted to request on "Nighttime." She would give Oregon pause for thought! What did she feel for him? Was she dazzled by a seduction that had occurred by default, simply because she was so lonely? Or was it deeper than that? She switched off the lights, climbed into bed, and turned on the radio. The red light from the dial glowed over the sheets as the familiar theme song filled the darkened bedroom. And then Rory Runyon was on.

Seven

"Welcome to 'Nighttime.' This is station KKZF, coming to you for the next two hours with your favorites, with music for the magic of midnight, soft mood music to lull you to sleep, to play in the background, to bring back memories." He spoke in mellow, drowsy tones that stroked her senses like strong, deft fingers.

Charity sighed and slithered down under the sheet. How could she not have known it was Oregon? Of course Rory and Oregon were the same. There was that marvelous voice that made Oregon's chest rumble slightly when he talked. The voice that was like melted butter oozing over every sensitive, quivering nerve. Rory Runyon had held her in his arms last night, kissed her! and made love to her! Charity blushed and tingled and ached and worried. Was she rushing into a relationship as swiftly as Ziza did?

And as disastrously? She shuddered at the memory of that year she had spent with Ziza, then shoved the memory aside, exchanging it for thoughts of Oregon.

"We'll start off tonight, darlin'," he was saying in his sexy voice, "with one just specially for you. This is to you. Here's 'Would You Be My Lady?'"

As the country music began, she wondered if he had chosen the song to send her a message in the title. Her heart thudded against her ribs.

As she listened to the song, her thoughts buzzed like busy little bees. Why hadn't Oregon told her he was Rory Runyon? Maybe he would tomorrow night. But she would teach him a lesson tonight! He had set her up last night, come home to a quivering mass of frustrated woman, and seduced her. And the memory turned her to jelly again.

The music ended. "There, darlin', did you like that? I hope so. Isn't this a marvelous night? Another nice evening like last night." His voice thickened, becoming so warm, so seductive. "Wasn't last night the best ever?" Charity sighed blissfully as he continued, "Tonight the temperature's seventy degrees, with a breeze and a full moon. Have you seen that moon? It's a big white pearl in the black sky. I'd like to sit in the moonlight and hold you in my arms. Would you like that, darlin'? Just sit and listen to the next song. How's this? 'You Oughta Be Home with Me'? Let's listen."

Soft music and Barry Manilow's voice drifted into the darkened room, and Charity bit her lip. Was Oregon/Rory playing these songs to tell her something? Or was she imagining that they might be for her? She listened to Oregon's chatter in between songs, and to two more records, "My One and Only" and "Waiting for You." Then he asked for requests.

She sat up, dialed frantically, and listened to the phone ring. His voice came over the radio and the phone. "Hi, there. This is Rory Runyon of 'Nighttime,' at station KKZF."

"Rory, this is Charity."

"Charity."

She slipped beneath the sheet and tried to catch her breath.

"Darlin', I'd hoped you'd call. What song would you like to hear?"

Sweet revenge. " 'The Men in My Life.' "

He coughed. " 'The Men in My Life'? That's an unusual request, but I'll play it for you. Don't go away, darlin'. Here's your request." The song began, and Oregon's throaty voice came over the wire. "Charity, you've been holding out on me. The men in your life—I thought I might be the *man* in your life."

She looked at the phone. Now, why couldn't he have said that to her last night when he held her close? Men were impossible to understand! "You are, Rory," she answered breathlessly, so full of sincerity she was struck by wonder at herself.

"I belong to a group?"

"No, it's just you."

"Then you should've requested 'The Man I Love,' or some song like that."

"Well, there's another man . . . but you're the one I really want to know."

"You're just saying that because it's safe."

"No, Rory, I'm not."

"Another man." He said it like a death knell. Like the voice of doom.

"I'd trade him for you." Now she was marching straight into deep water. Revenge? She might drown in the waters she stirred up.

"Darlin', I'm overcome! I'm just a voice in the night."

"Oh, but you're so sensitive, so . . . much more honest with me."

He coughed again. "Charity, I . . ."

She waited. And waited. The long red second hand on her clock swept on steadily. "Yes?" she finally said.

"Maybe you're judging him too harshly. Tell me about this other man in your life, darlin'."

Now *he* was treading on dangerous ground! "Well, Rory, I've met someone and I like the way he kisses."

There was a flurry of coughs. "Oh, darlin', you do?"

"Yes, but he still doesn't have what you do. Your sensitivity. I can talk to you. You talk to me. That's important. More important than spectacular kisses, don't you think?"

His voice was in the basement, down so low, it practically sent vibrations over the phone wires. "Damn, we're at the end of the song. Call me back, dar—"

As the music faded Charity grinned and wriggled her toes. Chalk one up for her, Mr. Oregon Brown. Put that in your noggin and think about it! It was the first time she had ever heard Oregon swear. Usually it was "Mercy" or "My!" or some other mild word. She smoothed the sheet as his voice came from the radio.

"There we have it, 'The Men in My Life.' Charity, darlin', you call in again, will you?"

"Sure, Rory."

"That's good. I'll be waiting. Don't forget me. Now, we'll take a little break here to talk about something scrumptious, Henrietta's Apple Pie Mix. Yu-um-yum."

Oregon's drawling "yum-yums" sent Charity's pulse into flight. In husky tones that sounded as seductive as his usual patter, he urged his listeners to try Henrietta's Pie Mix. "You want something that will melt in your mouth? That is so delicious you'll have to come back for more?" Charity wriggled. Henrietta should sell a whopping big amount of pie mix. "Just reach out and pick up Henrietta's Pie Mix the next time you're in the store."

Each word made her want to reach out for Oregon! He added softly, insinuatingly, "Oh, it's so tantalizing. Your taste buds will thank you. Just try Henrietta's Pie Mix and see for yourself. Don't take my word for it. Pick some up tomorrow.

"Now, ready for some music again? Here's another oldie. I've been waiting all day to play it. Are you listening, darlin'? Good, here goes." In a languorous voice he said, " 'Upstairs in My House.' "

"Upstairs in My House"! He was playing it to her for last night! It was a rock song by Men At Work and had a lively beat that wasn't going to put anyone to sleep. It wasn't typical of the music played on 'Nighttime.' He had to have chosen it for the title! Why was he so vocal as Rory Runyon and so evasive as Oregon Brown? Maybe he had a guilty conscience about setting her up for seduction last night!

The next song was a request from someone named Dinah. Charity lay in the dark and wondered what Oregon was saying to Dinah while the song played. How many women were in his life? How seriously had he been involved with one in his past? She knew so little about him. And so much. Her lashes fluttered closed while she thought about his kisses.

The song ended, and he played two more, titles that meant nothing to her. Maybe she had imagined the others were meant to convey a message to her. Then he asked for requests again. She sat up, dialed quickly, and felt her heart jump when he said, "Hi, there."

"Rory, it's me, Charity."

"Good, darlin. I'm so glad you called again. What would you like to hear now?"

" 'Why Do People Lie?' "

" 'Why Do People Lie?' Fine. You know, that'll wake everyone up, darlin'. That's a red-hot Kenny Loggins."

"I know. You won't play it?"

"It's coming right up now. Hang on to your seats out there. Here we go."

The heavy beat filled the room, and Charity held her breath.

"Charity. We're not on the air now. Darlin', no one should lie to you. I know just how sweet you are."

She slipped down in bed, cradling the phone between her ear and shoulder. It was hard to get her breath. "Thank you, Rory. You don't really know."

"Charity . . ."

And she knew he was on the brink of telling her again. And again he didn't.

"Yes?"

"Tell me some more about the man you like to kiss."

Her eyes flew open. Why wouldn't he admit his identity? Well, Mr. O. O. Brown would wish he had! "Well, I intend to get him out of my life quickly."

Two beats of silence followed her announcement, and then he said, "Is that so! You ought to give him more of a chance before you come to a conclusion."

"I've given him enough chances for a lifetime. He just doesn't have what you do, Rory. He doesn't tell me how he feels."

"Well, it's hard sometimes, Charity, for guys to put

their feelings into words. Sometimes they do things that make them feel guilty later and then it's hard to talk about it."

"You mean this guy feels guilty because he kissed me, so now he wishes he hadn't, but he can't admit he has regrets?"

"No! He couldn't have any regrets—Dammit, the record's over. Call me again."

He sounded frantic. Not one bit like his usual laid-back self. She smiled and listened as he changed to the familiar slow drawl. "There, darlin'. Everyone should be wide awake now. Darlin', call me again tonight, will you?"

"Sure, Rory."

"Good. Let's settle down with the next tune. Put your head back on a soft pillow, close your eyes, think of that special person, someone you want to be close to. Think of that certain someone in your life and listen to this next tune. It will help you relax. Here's 'Kisses Sweeter than Wine.' "

The music came on, and as she listened, her thoughts were on Oregon's smile, his green-and-gold-flecked eyes. Floating in a cloud of bliss, she listened to two more songs, a commercial done in Oregon's husky voice, which could sell furnaces in the Amazon, another request by a sultry-voiced female named Samantha, and more songs. Time ticked past. Samantha called in again. Charity didn't care for her deep, breathless voice at all. Finally the last chance for a request came over the air. Determined to beat Samantha, she dialed hastily and was gratified to hear the ring, then Oregon's husky voice. She was aching with longing for him. She wanted his kisses, his big strong arms, his loving. She wanted him to tell her he was Oregon Brown!

"Rory, this is Charity again."

"Charity, darlin', you stayed up until the end of the program. What do you want to hear?"

" 'All Alone Tonight.' "

" 'All Alone Tonight' it is. I wish you were here with me, darlin', so I could hold you close. Here's your song."

The music started and Oregon's voice came over the phone. "Charity?"

"Yes. I'm lonesome, Rory."

"Oh, darlin', if you only knew how lonely I am. I wish we could be together. I get so lonely . . ."

"Rory, isn't there anyone in your life?"

"No, darlin'. Except you."

"You tell everyone that."

"No, I don't. Charity, darlin', you don't know how lonesome I've been. I feel like a rolling stone. I don't belong any place, no one belongs to me."

He sounded sincere. Heartbreakingly sincere. She wondered about Oregon. How could anyone who seemed so self-assured, who had worked for one of the largest newspapers in the U.S., who had a nice house and so few apparent worries, be lonesome? There should be a flock of women in his life. The thought startled her. Oregon was appealing, sexy, intelligent, and such a magnificent lover!

"Charity, don't go away. Maybe you should give this guy a little time, a chance to talk to you."

"You don't want to be the one man in my life?"

"Oh, yeah, darlin'."

"Rory, there must be some woman in your life."

"Just you, darlin'. I think I'm falling in love with you."

"I might be falling in love with you." Was she?

"What about the guy who kisses so well?"

"He simply doesn't have what you do. We don't talk things over, we don't feel the same about life, the way you and I do. He doesn't have your . . . voice."

"Charity, we're going to have to meet."

She looked at the phone, then returned it to her ear. "Tomorrow?"

He chuckled softly. "Soon, darlin'. Real, real soon."

"I can't wait until tomorrow night."

Another tiny pause, then he asked, "Charity, are you going to listen to 'Nighttime' tomorrow night?"

"I wouldn't miss it for anything."

"Darlin', I won't—well—Hell, the music's over."

Now, what had he been about to say? She listened to his closing.

"Well, that wraps it up at station KKZF for tonight. Sleep well, darlin'. Nii-aight."

She melted. Then she turned off the radio, climbed out of bed, pulled on a robe, and stepped out onto the back porch. While she sat in the dark, staring at Oregon's house to watch for his light to come on, she wondered about him. Was he really so lonesome, or was that a line? Crickets chirped a shrill melody in the quiet night, while moonlight splashed over the flowers and yard. Finally Charity saw a light flicker on upstairs in Oregon's house, then off again. His room was downstairs, hidden by the board fence, but for a few seconds he had been in the bedroom where she had slept last night. She wished she were there again and was shocked at her feelings. How could she fall for Oregon so completely and quickly, when she had been so cautious with men in the past? There was no logical answer. Reluctantly she rose and went inside to bed.

Thursday morning the ringing of the phone woke her from a sound sleep. "Charity?"

It was Oregon, and he sounded just like Rory. If she hadn't known before, she would now. " 'Morning, Oregon."

"Darlin', you're in bed!" His voice lowered. "I can just picture you there, your curls all tangled, your blue eyes sleepy, your long, pale lashes curling over your eyes. Your mouth so inviting . . . I want you to wake me up, so we can love again."

He sure wasn't at a loss for words when he had a phone in his hand. His seductive voice stroked her, and she stretched sinuously in bed. "Enough of that!"

"You don't like it?"

She heard the hint of laughter in his voice. "Not now. It's disturbing."

"That's exactly what I want it to be, hon."

"Oregon!"

"My attorney says you've decided to sell the paper."

"That's right. I don't know anything about a newspaper. Aunt Mattie doesn't either. So I want to sell it. Yesterday I talked to our lawyer, Mr. Oppenheim, about selling."

"Well, I'm interested in buying. I want a paper. I can't get the ink out of my blood."

"I think we can work out a sale. I'd like you to have the paper. That would please Aunt Mattie. She sings your praises rather high."

"She's sweet. I'd like to hear someone else sing my praises."

She laughed. "You're cute."

"Oh, my. I don't care to be called 'cute.' I'll have to repair my image tonight."

"That was a compliment, not a challenge."

"Yeah, sure. Cute." He sounded disgusted. "Charity . . ."

"Yes?"

"It was better to wake up yesterday, with you in my arms." His voice was intimate and husky, sending dancing sparks cascading down her spine. She was breathless, yearning for him.

"Hmmm."

"Charity, I want to kiss you, to really kiss you."

"Hmmm."

His voice held a smile. "See you in a little while, darlin'."

"Hmmm." The receiver clicked in her ear. Bemused, she lay in bed while memories played through her mind like a kaleidoscope. Finally she dressed in cut-offs, a white cotton shirt, and sandals, and went to work to help clean the house thoroughly.

At about three in the afternoon, when she was in Aunt Mattie's hot attic above the garage, Oregon's head thrust through the opening in the attic floor and he grinned at her. "Hi. Want some help?"

Eight

She straightened, suddenly aware of the smudges of dust on her face and hands, of a sheen of perspiration on her brow, tangled locks curling over her forehead. She smiled. "You're just in time."

"Charity, is Mattie moving away?"

"I don't know what we'll do, so I'm trying to sort through things and get rid of what she doesn't want or need. She can't stay alone, but we haven't reached a decision about the future." She glanced around. "I don't know what to do with all this stuff. There are some heavy things that should go to the Salvation Army and I've been wondering how I would get them down out of the attic."

"At your service, darlin'." He scrambled up with ease and crouched slightly to avoid hitting his head on the sloping roof. Then, without hesitation, he reached for her.

"Oregon, it's too hot up here . . ."

"It sure is," he murmured as he leaned down to kiss her. His kiss was more overwhelming than the last had been, and it turned the attic into an inferno. Dimly she heard Aunt Mattie calling her name.

Oregon released her, and she answered. "Yes?"

"You're wanted on the phone. It's long distance, Charity. It's Ziza."

"I'm coming." She sounded as if she had run a mile. She pointed to Uncle Hubert's golf bag and clubs and a screen door, propped against the attic wall. "Can you bring those down, please?"

"Sure thing."

She hurried down the steps and discovered Aunt Mattie had pulled the phone around the corner from the kitchen counter to the garage. It rested on the washing machine. When Charity answered, Ziza's voice came over the crackling wire.

"Charity, sweetie, this is Ziza." Charity could picture Ziza's wild tangle of black curls, her big blue eyes, and the slender figure that made people think she was ten years younger than her age. "Sweetie, I'm married to the most adorable man! This is finally it, Charity, forever! Bernard. I just can't wait for you to meet him." She didn't pause for a remark from Charity, but continued breathlessly, with laughter punctuating her sentences. "Sweetie, you're not married yet, are you?"

"No, Ziza."

"Are you in love?"

"No . . ."

"Well, sweetie, it's high time we changed that! You're too cute and too old to live without a man. And I have just the one for you. Mr. Perfect."

"Ziza, I don't need to meet any men." She saw a

long black boot emerge from the attic and rest on the top step. She picked up the phone to step inside the kitchen, but the cord got twisted and she couldn't untangle it without dropping the phone.

"Don't be ridiculous! You need a man in your life more than anything else, and I'd be remiss in my duty if I didn't see to it that you got one."

Charity felt as if she were standing in quicksand. Sinking in quicksand. Mired to her waist in oozing trouble. Both boots came down a step and long, jeaned legs began to appear. She knew Oregon could hear every word she said.

"Ziza, please, I'm living the way I want to."

"I can't hear you. We have a damn poor connection. You'll love him. It's Bernard's brother, Rolf. He's a dreamboat. Who's your favorite actor?"

"I don't have one. Ziza, don't bring him to meet me. I can't go out with him."

"Why not? There is someone else!"

Charity was aware of Oregon standing behind her. "No, there isn't!"

"Then you'll love Rolf and you need to meet him."

"Ziza, I don't have time to date. I have to take care of Mattie." She glanced around. Oregon was investigating Uncle Hubert's golf clubs, studying them intently.

"That's all the more reason to get you out. Rolf looks just like . . . hold your breath . . . Christopher Reeve!"

Charity's patience snapped. "If he looks so damned much like Christopher Reeve, why does he need you to introduce him to a woman?"

The minute she said it, she wanted to clamp her hand over her mouth. Oregon's head raised, and he stopped all pretense of studying anything except her.

He grinned. She felt her cheeks burning beneath his gaze.

"I had to do some arm twisting," Ziza answered, unperturbed. "You'll faint when you see him. If I weren't so in love with Bernard . . . and a teensy bit older than Rolf . . . well, you wouldn't lay eyes on him!" Ziza laughed.

"Don't invite him to meet me, Ziza. When will you and Bernard get here?"

"We're in Houston now, and we'll get in about noon Saturday. We'll stay at a motel, sweetie, but Rolf will stay with you, and don't protest. Mattie has already said he can stay. And you have a date Saturday night."

"No, I don't."

"Why not? Sweetie, are you in love? I think you're in love! Don't deny it, I can tell. Charity, who is he?"

A silence ensued while Charity mulled over the best answer to give her aunt. "I'm not alone, Ziza."

"Mattie's there?"

"Well, no. A neighbor is."

"Charity, you sound different. It won't hurt you to tell me who the lucky man is. Mattie and her neighbor will be delighted."

"I can't talk about it now."

Oregon had folded his arms across his chest and planted his feet apart while he gazed at her thoughtfully.

Ziza laughed uproariously. "Prim and proper Charity. Come on, I can imagine your blush and the little ladies' giggles. Tell me who the man is or I'll have to ask Mattie."

"You're right, Ziza, I'm prim. Let's discuss it later. Just visit Rolf in Oklahoma City on your way home

and forget about introducing us." She was on fire.
Damn Oregon anyway!

"Charity, come on. I won't be satisfied until you tell
me who he is."

Now she had put herself between a slab of marble
and a block of concrete. Either way she was up
against solid trouble. She didn't want to meet Rolf, to
have him for a houseguest, yet she didn't dare tell
Ziza that she was in love with Oregon. She raised her
chin and faced Oregon defiantly. "Ziza, there isn't
anyone I'm in love with, but I don't want a blind date
with Rolf!"

And she knew that the moment she'd declared she
wasn't in love, she had flung a challenge at Oregon.
He started toward her with a gleam in his eye that
told her exactly what he intended. Her heart thudded
against her rib cage and her pulse went into high
gear.

And Ziza's happy voice came over the wire loudly
enough for Oregon to hear. "Oh, Charity, I wonder! I
can imagine your blush. Are the ladies giggling?"

Oregon pushed the phone away from her mouth,
bent down, and kissed her. His arms went around
her waist and he pulled her to him, kissing her as
passionately and as hard as possible.

She fought, but there was no way to combat arms
like steel bands, a chest like granite, and a kiss like a
roaring fire.

She did the only thing she could think to do under
the circumstances. She hung up on Ziza. And
Oregon kept right on kissing her until she felt she
would faint. She trembled, she ached, she struggled,
and she couldn't resist—she kissed him in return.
Fervently. She forgot Ziza, Rolf, her anger, everything

in the world except Oregon Brown. Adorable, sexy, tongue-tied Oregon Oliver Brown.

The phone rang. And rang and rang. Finally she realized it and reached behind her, struggling again to pull free of Oregon's embrace.

He relented, raising his head. She brought the phone to her ear while she stared into his burning eyes.

"Hello? Charity? What happened?"

Charity tried to wriggle free. Oregon grinned and leaned down to nibble her earlobe. "We . . . got cut off. Oh, don't!"

"Don't what? What's the matter with you? You sound breathless."

"It's a . . . poor connection." She couldn't think. She felt tingles coursing through her. Oregon's tongue touched her ear as she struggled to get away from him.

"Now, Charity, it's all set. You have a dinner date Saturday night with Rolf. Is there a good restaurant in Enid?"

"Red Lobster," Oregon said.

"Charity, is there a man with you?"

"A man? Whatever makes you think that?"

"I can't hear you."

"I said, Red Lobster is a good place to eat." She covered the mouthpiece of the phone and whispered frantically, "Get away! Stop that, Oregon!"

"Go out to dinner with me Saturday night." His chin thrust forward slightly, and his green eyes glinted with determination.

"I can't, Oregon," she whispered. She couldn't let Ziza get hold of Oregon. There wouldn't be a minute's peace, and Ziza would ruin their relationship. What relationship? an inner voice scoffed.

"I can't, Oregon," she whispered.

"Charity, sweetie, is someone with you?"

"Go out with me."

"No." She said it to both of them, speaking into the phone while she looked Oregon in the eye.

He folded his arms across his chest and rocked on his heels.

"You sound different, sweetheart."

"It's the connection."

Suddenly Oregon's fingers closed over the phone, and he took it from her so swiftly, she couldn't stop him. While his eyes warned her to leave him alone, his deep voice said, "Hi, Ziza, this is Oregon."

Charity felt as if the quicksand had closed over her head. There went Rolf, peace of mind, Oregon, the weekend, her life. When Ziza got her teeth into a man, she didn't let go.

"I'm a neighbor of Mattie's and I have a date with Charity Saturday night."

Charity couldn't hear Ziza's reply, but she saw Oregon grin. An eyelid dropped over one eye in a quick wink that didn't do anything to soothe her anger.

"That's right, Ziza. Why don't you save old Rolf the trip if you can see him in Oklahoma City?" Another pause, a wider grin appeared, with dimples, and then he said, "Sure thing. See you Staurday. I'll tell Charity and give her a kiss for you." He replaced the receiver and smiled smugly at Charity.

"You just did the lowest, sneakiest—"

That one damned eyebrow climbed into an arch, and his eyes were filled with devilish glitter as he interrupted her. "I'm not about to let you go out with a guy named Rolf who looks like Christopher Reeve.

You didn't want to go anyway. Come here. I'm supposed to give you a kiss for Ziza."

She flung her hands up to forestall him. "I didn't want to tell Ziza about you either!"

"So I noticed. Not in love, huh?"

"Now, Oregon, you don't know my aunt, but you will by Saturday night. Oh, brother, you will!" Charity was tempted to add that Ziza was probably planning a wedding right now. Heat burned up from her toes as Oregon pulled her to him and kissed her again. Kissed her as thoroughly and as fantastically as before. When he released her, she stared at him for long, long seconds until she remembered what she had been doing. "I've got work to do," she said.

"I came along just in time to save you from disaster and I'm not worried about your Aunt Ziza. And you're not in love, huh?"

"I had to tell her that." She was blushing furiously and felt aggravated by his high-handed tactics.

He brushed her nose with his finger and drawled, "Well, we'll see about that, darlin'. And we have a dinner date Saturday night."

"I have to clean the attic, and I can get along without your help, Oregon."

He grinned. "Now, don't get in a huff with me. I didn't come over here for that."

"I'm not in a huff. I'm going back to work, and I don't need any help."

His grin widened. "That isn't what you said a few minutes ago."

"I'm saying it now." She climbed the steps to the attic, aware that he was probably watching every movement. She thrust her head through the opening and saw the screen door lying on the floor, blocking her way. She couldn't climb up unless she stepped on the screen or lifted it down. And damned if she would ask for his help. She pulled the door toward her and lifted one end. The door was heavy and awkward to handle.

She heard a deep chuckle; then an arm closed around her waist. Oregon was standing on the steps as he reached up and lifted her off. For an instant, as he swung her around, she thought they'd fall. Then he settled back against the steps, holding her against his big, long body. She rested her hands on his shoulders and looked into his eyes, and knew she had lost the battle completely.

"My, are you a dirty fighter," she murmured.

"We weren't fighting. Not for one second." He leaned forward and kissed her. His arm held her tightly against him while his other hand cupped the back of her head.

He spread his legs slightly, and her toes rested on a step. It was higher than the one on which Oregon stood, and put her face on the same level as his. And fitted her body to his seductively. Held so tightly against him, she felt his arousal, his growing need for her. His tongue met hers in a delicious tangle that sent her heart flying for an eternity before she reluctantly pushed away. They looked into each other's eyes, and she wondered what he was thinking. She thought he was marvelous. And she refused to think about what would happen when Ziza discovered him. "I'd better go," she whispered.

"For now," he answered, and released her, helping her down before turning and easily lifting down the screen door.

"When will Ziza arrive?" he asked.

"Saturday." The mere thought made her nervous.

"Oregon, we've gotten rid of Rolf. Let's postpone our date until Ziza and Bernard are gone."

He grinned at her, and her heart sank. He was going to be as devilish as Old Nick himself. "She's part of your family, darlin'. I might as well meet her now."

Meet her now? What did Oregon mean by that? "Oregon . . . Never mind. Before you go, will you carry that door to the front? I need to take down the storm door and put up the screen."

"I'll do it."

He left, whistling a jolly tune, and she sat down on the bottom step. She felt as if she were lost in a fog. She couldn't handle Oregon at all. He had caused mountains of trouble in her life. And Ziza would come into their lives like Hurricane Hilda. And what would happen tonight with Oregon? What did she want to happen? One thing would occur—Oregon would be forced to admit he was Rory Runyon. Tonight he would have to explain his reasons for going to the station.

Five hours later, seated in Oregon's living room, Charity wondered what had happened to her plans. Nothing had gone the way she'd expected. She had dressed in a pale blue cotton sundress and sandals and been thrilled by Oregon's reaction when he opened the door. His green eyes had devoured her, drifting slowly down to her toes, up again over her hips and breasts, and down. She realized it was the first time he had seen her in a dress. Then he had helped Aunt Mattie inside and they had settled in the living room for a cocktail.

Dinner was served in the dining room by a maid, who left shortly after the dishes were done. Charity then expected Aunt Mattie to go home to bed and Oregon to go to work. Neither happened.

Aunt Mattie had napped all afternoon after the phone call from Ziza and was ready to enjoy the evening out. Oregon seemed in no hurry to go anywhere. Charity had a suspicion Oregon also had expected Aunt Mattie to go home early.

They chatted about first one thing, then another, while Oregon, looking too appealing for words, in navy slacks and a white shirt, lounged in a large, comfortable armchair. Aunt Mattie told them about her early childhood in Alva, Oklahoma, then about moving to Enid in the early days after statehood.

Charity couldn't believe that Aunt Mattie was so alert. It was the first night since her arrival that her aunt had stayed up past eight o'clock. Charity glanced continually at the clock over the mantel, watching it grow later and later. Still Oregon made no move to go to the station.

Eleven o'clock came, unheard-of for Aunt Mattie, yet the eyes behind the trifocals were as bright as ever. By eleven-thirty Charity knew it was too late for Oregon to get to the station. She rose. "Aunt Mattie, it'll be midnight soon. . . ."

"Midnight! Imagine that! You sweet children have been so entertaining. I haven't been up this late in years. Oh, dear, we've kept you up late, Oregon."

He grinned. "That's all right, Mattie. I don't turn in early, and I can catch forty winks tomorrow." He looked at Charity. "How's your insomnia, Charity? Have you slept any better the past few nights?"

"I don't have insomnia." She blushed and hated it.

"She just stays up all hours and rises with the sun," Mattie said.

"That so?" His green eyes started to twinkle. "The last sunrise I saw was the best I've ever seen."

Charity headed for the door, hoping Oregon would stop. "Wait a minute, Mattie," he said. "You forgot your purse." He handed it to her.

"Oh, my. I'd leave my head if it weren't attached. Charity is so good to remind me about things. Isn't she sweet, Oregon?"

"She's adorable."

Charity felt another wave of heat rush up from her throat. As she looked up at Oregon, her heart was throbbing and it was difficult to speak. "Thank you. That's nice."

He smiled and gave her quick wink. "Sweet Charity. It's almost time for the radio program you like."

"So it is. Do you always listen to 'Nighttime'?"

"No, but I catch it now and then."

They each took one of Mattie's elbows to help her down the steps to the car. Oregon closed the door after she was seated. As they started around the back of the car, Oregon's hand closed on Charity's arm.

"I thought we'd be alone a little while tonight," he whispered.

"She took a nap today so she could stay awake and visit with you." They stopped behind the back fender of the passenger side of the car, and Oregon slipped his arm around her waist, leaning down to kiss her.

It was a kiss that made her want dozens more. As she pushed away, she felt the intense longing that he stirred so easily.

"Oregon, Aunt Mattie will look for me."

"She won't mind if she sees me kiss you."

"Well, I don't want a bunch of questions."

"I'll be happy to answer them for you," he said complacently. "We kiss because we're falling in love."

"You know, you have moments when you're so damned arrogant, it's revolting!"

Suddenly he yanked her to his chest and kissed her again. Kissed her soundly until she returned it with just as much abandon. And, just as abruptly as he had reached for her, he released her. As she almost fell against the car, he said, "I rest my case."

"Damned arrogance!" she snapped, making him laugh softly.

He dropped his arm across her shoulders and walked her around the car, then reached for her door. For an instant before he opened it, he leaned close to her ear. "I wish you were stretched out on my black satin sheets. You were meant for them and for me, Charity Jane Webster!"

"Oregon, stop that!" she said, but her protest was too breathless to sound sincere. Trying to speak firmly, she said, "Thank you for the dinner." She tried again, hoping the breathy quality would vanish. "It was marvelous."

"You're welcome. Saturday night there'll be just the two of us and it'll be better."

"You may be jumping to the wrong conclusion."

"We need to be alone to talk, Charity."

"Well, I can't now. I better go. Aunt Mattie's waiting."

" 'Night, darlin'." There went her pulse. What a voice the man had!

" 'Night, Oregon." She climbed into the car and drove around the corner to Aunt Mattie's, her thoughts on Oregon's dynamite kisses, his sexy, sexy voice.

As soon as they were in the house, she went to her room to turn on 'Nighttime.' And, right on cue, Oregon's husky voice came over the air. She gazed at the radio and guessed the program was prerecorded. While she listened, she undressed, pulled on her nightgown and lay frowning in the darkness, missing Rory/Oregon's chatter and phone conversations, worried about Ziza, about Oregon. What did she feel for Oregon? Was it mere lust because of loneliness? Or was it deeper? And did it matter to him? Was it casual, a one-night stand, or had he spoken the truth on the phone when he'd said he was lonely and falling in love with her?

"Dammit," she whispered. Why didn't Oregon discuss things with her instead of teasing and aggravating her, and making her melt? He wasn't at a loss for words as Rory Runyon!

She turned off the radio and flounced onto her side. She lay facing a south window, and through it she saw a light blink in Oregon's house, on, then off. What was he doing? Was he lonesome now?

She groaned and turned onto the other side, squeezing her eyes closed, determined to put Oregon Oliver Brown out of her thoughts.

She failed miserably and slept only a few hours before sunshine awakened her to a bright Friday morning.

She dressed, cooked breakfast, then left to spend an hour with Mr. Oppenheim, going over papers and talking about the sale of the newspaper.

Then she had errands to run. Go to the County Health Department for a death certificate, go to the bank, buy groceries, fill the car with gas, get Aunt Mattie's prescription filled, and take Aunt Mattie to the doctor. She spent the entire day away from home and didn't see Oregon at all. And missed him terribly. It was five o'clock when she and Aunt Mattie returned home for dinner and found a note from Oregon tucked into the door. He had come over during the afternoon to see if he could help with anything. Charity was very disappointed that she had missed him.

Aunt Mattie was exhausted after their hectic day, so they ate an early dinner, and then Aunt Mattie went to bed.

Charity cleaned the house, then baked a cake and made a lime-Jell-O salad for Zizi and Bernard's visit. Finally she bathed and settled in bed to listen to 'Nighttime.'

Oregon's baritone came over the air, floating in the dark, bringing his presence into the bedroom. She could see green-gold eyes, imagine his big hands holding a record, see his long body relaxed in the chair, his tight jeans molding his strong legs.

She groaned softly and turned to stare at the radio. Tomorrow night they had a real, bona fide date. Would Oregon reveal his double identity then? The thought of a whole evening alone with Oregon was tantalizing.

"Hello, there, darlin'. I'm so glad you tuned in. This is Rory Craig Runyon at station KKZF bringing you 'Nii-aighttime.' Settle back, darlin'. For the next two hours you'll listen to slow, easy music, old favorites for late hours."

After a commercial, Oregon played "One Love in My Lifetime." Well, now, she didn't believe that was a message to her! No man like Oregon could have lived in a vacuum all these years. She checked over her list of carefully chosen requests: "Blue for You," "Say the Words," "Amazed and Confused," "I've Never Been a Woman Before." As she listened to the music she debated which song to request first.

The song ended, and Oregon's voice filled the room and her senses like an intoxicating sweet wine. She closed her eyes and thought of lying in Oregon's strong arms, of his gorgeous body so warm against hers. He played "Someday We'll Be Together," then asked for requests. Charity dialed quickly, but received a busy signal. Aggravated, she listened to Samantha's breathless voice, the same Samantha who had called in before! She requested "The Voice of Love," a song Charity didn't know but wished she had found first. She flounced down on the pillows to listen to the music and wonder if Oregon was talking to Samantha while the music played. Her eyes narrowed. She licked her lips and dialed the station. A recording came on the line. "Good evening. This is station KKZF, broadcasting to you at one thousand on your dial. If you wish to talk to someone at the station, you may leave a message at the sound of a beep. We will be open at eight o'clock in the morning. Thank you for calling KKZF."

Charity replaced the receiver without waiting to hear the beep. They must put the calls through to Oregon when he asked for requests, then switch back to the recording. She bit her lip. Was Oregon chatting with Samantha?

The song ended, and she let out her breath. "Goodbye, Samantha," she whispered, and listened carefully to Oregon's farewell.

"There you are, Samantha, a late-night song to soothe away the worries of the day. You call again, you hear?"

"I will, Rory," came the whispery female voice.

Well, he hadn't called Samantha "darlin'." "Here's our next, 'Only You,'" he said. "It's for you, darlin'. I'll listen and think about you, about your tempting lips and your big, beautiful eyes. Listen to the song."

Charity did. Was Oregon thinking about her? She

wriggled in the bed and thought about him, about his strength, his tenderness and passion. The cock-eyed, crooked smile and arch of brow that could be so devilish or so delightful. "Oregon!" she whispered. Tomorrow night—what would happen? At the thought her pulse jerked and rattled like an over-heated motor. Then Oregon was on again. "How's that? Nice song, wasn't it? Darlin', here's something else nice. Remember Henrietta's Pie Mix? Well, now we have Henrietta's Batter. You talk about yummy, scru-umptious, mouth-waterin' biscuits . . ."

Each word dropped on Charity's trembling nerves like sizzling oil. What a voice the man had! What a voice, and body, and kisses . . . "Oregon!" She wished she could conjure him up out of the darkness.

She listened raptly while he described biscuits in adjectives that made her quiver.

"Now let's get back to some music. What would you like to hear? You call and tell me, darlin' . . ."

Charity did, as rapidly as possible. She let out her breath with satisfaction as she listened to the ring, then heard Oregon's voice continue its magic.

"Rory, it's Charity."

"Darlin', I'm glad you called. Are you all right?"

"Fine," she lied. What would he do if she answered honestly?

"What song would you like to hear, darlin'?"

She blushed with such intensity she felt she must be glowing like the red dial on the radio. " 'I've Never Been a Woman Before,' " she said.

" 'I've Never Been a Woman Before,' " he repeated, sounding thoughtful. "That's an interesting title. Here it is, darlin'. Just for you."

The music began, then Oregon said, "Charity?"

"Yes."

"Darlin', I've been waiting for you to call me. 'I've Never Been a Woman Before'—did the guy you like to kiss cause this request?"

"He might have."

"I'm green with jealousy."

"You don't need to be. Not at all."

"I do if he's the reason you requested this song. Are . . . Charity, are you in love with him?"

"No. I can't love him, because he won't talk to me like you do. Not at all. I don't think he really likes me. I think he's just amusing himself."

"You're wrong. Oh, Charity, have you really talked to this guy?"

"Yes, I have." She glared into the darkness and glanced out the window at Oregon's dark house.

"Charity, I'll bet he's falling in love with you. He can't resist. He wouldn't want to resist."

"He doesn't act like it!"

"He doesn't act like it?" Shock and disbelief came through clearly.

"I guess he acts like it, but he doesn't *say* anything!"

"Give him time."

"Time! Rory, you wouldn't need time. You say the nicest . . ." She hesitated. What was good for the goose . . . Lowering her voice, she said breathlessly, "You say the sexiest things, really sexy, that excite me so much . . ."

"Dammit, Charity. How can I do a show when you say things like that in a voice that makes me turn into a bonfire?"

Elation tweaked her nerves. Score another for me, Oregon Brown! "Serves you right."

"Darlin', I just go home to an empty house. I don't

have anyone to love. I don't have anybody to talk to either."

"You have a goat—" The instant Charity said it, two things happened at once.

Nine

First, she clamped her hand over her mouth. Second, the record ended.

"Charity, you know!"

"Oregon, you're on the air, or you should be!"

"All that damned talk about—How long have you known?"

" 'Nighttime' isn't broadcasting?"

"Dammit, answer me!"

"We can't talk now!"

"Dammit!" And the last "dammit" was broadcast by "Nighttime." It came out clearly in Rory Runyon/Oregon Brown's voice. There was a screech, the jarring screech of a needle slipping across a record, and then "La Cucaracha" in all its snapping glory came blaring into the bedroom. Charity hung up. She didn't want to talk to Oregon right now. It did serve him right, but she wished she hadn't blurted the truth out over the phone! She would have preferred to discuss it with him in person, but it was too late now. Curiosity wracked her. Would he ask for another request when "La Cucaracha" finished? He must have snatched up the first record he could find.

She waited to see what would happen. Without a word from Rory Runyon another song, "Cuanto Le Gusta," followed. Charity bit her lip. Was he not talking because he was so angry? What was he doing? The music ended and another Spanish song started. Charity sat up. Had she wiped out Rory Runyon's career as a disc jockey? What was Oregon doing?

The music finally ended and a male voice came over the air. A male voice that was pleasant, but a pitch higher than and definitely not Rory Runyon's!

"There, did you like that touch from south of the border? A little bit of Spanish? This is Bill Foster, filling in for Rory Runyon. Rory will be back tomorrow night, folks, with his usual patter. . . ."

Charity blinked. Where was Oregon? Her eyes widened. There was only one place he could be! He was on his way to her house! She threw aside the covers and scrambled out of bed to find her robe. She pulled it on with shaking fingers, trying to figure how much time had lapsed since she had talked with him.

Something thumped against the window. In shock she stared at the window a second, then rushed to open it. Moonlight bathed Oregon in a silvery glow. He stood beyond the patio, his fists on his hips, his feet spread apart, golden curls tumbling over his forehead.

"Charity, come out here."

She went. He sounded as if he would come right through the window if she argued.

As she hurried through the house, she tied her belt

securely around her waist and buttoned the collar to her chin. Her pulse raced and she felt alternately hot and cold. He sounded angry, but he didn't have any more right to anger than she did. He was the one who had hidden his identity!

She closed the door behind her and found him on the patio. It was dark beneath the sloping roof and difficult at first to see his eyes.

"How long have you known?" he asked gruffly.

"Why didn't you admit it to me?" she countered.

"Dammit, you've just been leading me along!"

"Listen here, Oregon Brown! Talk about 'leading me along'! You're the one who started the deception! Why didn't you tell me the truth right away?"

"Because you sounded so convinced that Rory Runyon was nicer than Oregon Brown."

Stunned, she peered at him, leaning closer to try to seen his green eyes. "I don't believe you for a second!" She remembered that night at his house. "You wouldn't tell me because you deliberately tried to get me ready and aching for you so you could come home and seduce me! Deny it, Oregon!"

He shuffled his feet and gently grasped her shoulders. "Charity . . ."

It was true. She had known it all along, but it hurt to hear him hesitate. Her eyes had adjusted to the darkness, and she detected a flush creeping over his cheeks.

"Charity, I did, honey, but I can't say I'm sorry, because I'm not. Then I was afraid you'd be angry with me if I told you. When did you guess?"

"That night."

"You knew that night. . . . Well, damn!" He let go of her. "You've been stringing me along on the show."

"It wasn't as bad as what you did!"

His voice changed completely. The embarrassment vanished to be replaced by a cocky self-assurance that was becoming more and more familiar to her. "You really like the way I kiss?"

"Now, Oregon, I said some of that to get revenge." It was her turn to blush.

"Oh, sure. Let's see, what did you request? You wanted 'I've Never Been a Woman Before,' 'Touch Me in the Morning' . . ."

"I know what songs I requested!" she snapped.

"And you like the way I kiss. You like to talk to Rory. You're falling in love with Rory. You know, you have a little sneakiness yourself. You really had me going!"

"Oregon, I'd better go inside." She was beginning to get signals of danger ahead. Big danger.

He leaned back against the door, facing her, and ran his hands lightly up and down her arms. Her alarm system rang and clanged in a flurry of warnings, but it was too late. Much too late. Her gaze drifted down over his blue cotton shirt and his tight jeans, stretched taut by his arousal. She swallowed with difficulty and raised her eyes to find him watching her intently. His big fingers slipped up her arms, over her shoulders, to her throat.

His husky voice lowered, and she started to melt. "You like the way I kiss, you like to talk to me. Well, it's mutual. I like to talk to you. I like to kiss you. Darlin', I really like to kiss you. Miss Charity Jane Webster, I'm in love with you!" Wrapping his arms around her, he pulled her close and kissed her. And she thawed like snow before a fire, anger dissolving into eagerness. His tongue slipped into her mouth, touching hers in wave after wave of stormy, scalding surges, exploring her textures, the moistness beneath her tongue, the yielding softness of her inner lips.

She was dimly aware when he scooped her into his arms and entered the house. His footsteps were muffled by the thick carpet as he carried her to her room. He pushed the door closed behind them and set her on her feet, continuing to kiss her until all her fragmented thoughts and doubts had disappeared and all she knew was how badly she wanted him. His kisses were heady, sweet wine, intoxicating and delicious, sending her senses on a spiral of desire.

She locked her arms around his neck and clung to him, twining her fingers in his hair, feeling his hard maleness press against her as if there were no clothing between them. One hand slipped across his broad, firm shoulders down to the buttons of his shirt. She twisted the button free, slipping her fingers beneath the smooth cotton to his furred chest.

He caught her face in his hands. His voice was hoarse, so low and breathless she felt as if each word was a physical contact. "Charity, I love you."

"Oh, Oregon!" Her heart pounded fiercely. She loved hearing him say the words, yet it threw her into a turmoil. Then her thoughts faded like fog on an Oklahoma spring morning, melted away by the sunlight in his green-gold eyes.

He stepped back and slowly untied her belt, tugging it free. The belt slipped from her waist and dropped. Then he started on the buttons. His knuckles brushed her flesh, his eyes holding her imprisoned. As tension built, making her quiver like a young willow in a windstorm, Oregon slowly unbuttoned the blue robe and finally pushed it over her shoulders and let it drop around her ankles on the floor.

"You're mine, Charity," he said in his sexy, husky voice, which gloved a note of steel. "Mine forever. I won't let you go."

Charity lay sprawled on Oregon's big, warm body, her cheek on his chest, her legs pressed against his. She listened to his heart thump, to his breath gradually slow, while his hands stroked her bare back, trailing lightly, comfortably down over the rise and fall of her curves, over her buttocks, to the back of her legs, then up again to her shoulders. And at last, Oregon Brown could talk as well as Rory Runyon!

"Charity, darlin', how I've wanted to do that, to hold you again and love you. Darlin', that first night . . . after we made love I couldn't admit I was Rory. And I couldn't apologize, because I wasn't sorry. Not one damn bit! There weren't any regrets. Charity, you and I were meant to be. We just are. There's a chemistry between us, isn't there, darlin'?"

"Hmmm, Oregon." She couldn't talk. She was exhausted, floating in a cotton-candy euphoria, in a sweet world of frothy pink that blanked out everything else. Oregon, Oregon, Oregon! Rory Runyon! Rory Runyon wasn't as important as Oregon Brown. Oregon Brown was the world. Completely. She sighed with contentment.

"Charity, you're mighty quiet."

"Hmmmm." Satisfaction oozed in her response.

His fingertips drifted down, down lightly as feathers to touch her intimately.

She stirred. "Hmmmm, Oregon!"

"I thought I might get a response. What happened to your conversation?" He sounded amused, but she felt too filled with lethargy to move and look at him. She twined chest curls around her fingers, then blew at them. "Oregon, I can't talk now. I can't talk when I'm very passionate—or when I'm exhausted." She felt doubly exhausted after the effort to explain.

He chuckled, a deep, throaty sound that always made her tingle. "I love you, little Charity. Love you terribly. You're all I want." He shifted, then looked down at her. His fingers tangled in her curly hair, twisting it lightly.

"Charity, marry me."

Ten

Her eyes opened wide, her heart started thudding, and her breath stopped.

"Darlin', marry me. Charity Jane Webster, I want you to share my life forever. To have and to hold from this day forward. Will you marry me?"

Her euphoria vanished. She was stunned, blinded by his dazzling proposal. And at the same time frightened.

He sounded so confident, so absolutely sure of himself as he said, "You're all I want."

"Oregon . . ." She didn't know what to say. His eyes, such a deep, deep emerald green, focused intently on her. He blinked, and his brows drew together.

"What is it, darlin'?"

"Oregon, I'm falling in love with you. I *do* love you, but let's not rush into marriage."

"Oh, my lord. Charity Jane Webster, you look like the kind of woman who would want nothing but marriage. What's the hang-up?"

"It's Ziza," she answered, totally alert now.

"Well, she doesn't have to live with us. She doesn't have to give you permission, either!"

"Oregon, try to understand. My mother died when I was fifteen years old. Dad lived just eight months longer and was killed in an accident at a railroad crossing. His car was hit by a train. I was sent to live with Ziza for a year, then spent the next three years with Aunt Mattie and Uncle Hubert. That year with Ziza was so terrible. She divorced her fifth husband, began to date, and married the sixth. Bernard is husband number eight."

Oregon's mouth curled up in a grin. "Darlin', you aren't going to have eight."

"It's not funny, Oregon. I don't want to rush into marriage. I really didn't want to rush into an affair. I promised myself when I was sixteen that I'd never live like Ziza. She dotes on men and attracts them like cherry blossoms attract bees. I hated that year. She went with three men before she married again. She and my mother were sisters, but they were as different as sugar and salt."

He sobered and brushed the curls off her damp forehead. "Hon, you were young, hurt over the loss of your parents, suffering growing pains. That made everything worse. Charity, you won't be like your aunt. You won't have eight husbands."

"No, I certainly won't! I want one. One and only." She focused on Oregon again. "I just don't want to rush into something. Give me time, Oregon." As he gazed down at her in silence, something tightened inside Charity. She felt torn between years' of promising herself to be careful, to be very sure, and a desperate longing to accept his proposal now. She twined her arms around his neck. "Don't be angry. I love you, Oregon, but we've haven't known each other any time at all!"

"Time isn't what counts," he said solemnly. "Charity, I love to hear you say you love me. I want to hear it every day."

"Just give us a little time. It counts some. You don't know me at all and I don't know you."

"You mean you don't know me as well as you want to. I know you, darlin'. Remember, your aunt and uncle talked about you a lot. I know that you won a drama award your junior year in college; I know you hurt your ankle once when you were a cheerleader; I know your first contract in the landscaping business was with Char-burg Drive-in; I know you have hay fever—"

"Well, I don't know anything about you! For all I know, you've had three wives."

"Nope. None."

"Were you ever engaged?"

"Yep, once."

"Why didn't you get married?"

"I guess I didn't want to because I kept thinking of reasons to put it off, until she finally gave me an ultimatum and we broke up."

She narrowed her eyes and stared at him intently. "How long had you known her when you proposed?"

"Four years." She thought she detected a twinkle in his eyes.

"Dammit, Oregon, you take advantage of me!" she said without anger.

"Oh, sure. Maybe I did once."

"There are so many problems. You don't know . . ." Her voice trailed away.

He leaned down to kiss her forehead, her cheek, her ear. He whispered, "What don't I know?"

"Well, I have to decide what to do about Aunt Mattie. I don't think she can live alone. She forgets too many things. And there's my business. Oregon, my landscape business failed and I have debts up to my chin."

"I have money up to my chin." He pulled back a little and grinned.

"My, what modesty!" Her smiled vanished, and she frowned. "Seriously, you're not going to pay my debts."

"Oh, lord. I've fallen in love with an independent woman."

"Too bad, buster," she said flippantly, then sobered. "Really, Oregon, I have to get a job and pay off the debts. I don't know what kind of employment I can find. I have a degree in landscape architecture."

His dimples deepened and his green eyes glinted as he said, "Darlin', you worry too much. Way too much. Your problems aren't that big and I'm happy to share them."

"Wait until you have to share Ziza," she said darkly, while her thoughts seethed. Oregon wanted to marry her! To be with her forever. She stroked his broad shoulder. "Oregon, don't push. I can't resist much pressure, but we haven't known each other long and I'm trying to keep my promise to myself. I'm trying to be sensible."

He kissed her throat, then drifted to her ear again. "Okay, darlin'. Be sensible, take your time, but don't ask me to dally long. I want you, Charity, and I'm

going to have you. You'll be Mrs. Oregon Brown someday. And not in the distant future!"

His words came out in a breathy warmth over her
ear, words said in his sexiest voice. She tingled and
tightened her arms around him.

"This wasn't something taken lightly, Charity."
Suddenly Oregon sounded vulnerable, almost
pained.

"Are you really lonesome?"

"Darlin', you're what I need in my life." He leaned
forward, his arms slipping beneath her to hold her.

"Now, Oregon, I think you have a gleam in your
eye."

"Darn right I do. Come here, darlin'. I'll fill your
thoughts until all you know is me. Absolutely. I want
to hold you and kiss you and touch your beautiful
body. To feel you respond, to feel you tremble in my
arms, to listen to your heart pound for me." His voice
was Rory Runyon's seductive best. And it worked its
sensual magic on her ready and all too willing body.
She raised her mouth for his kiss and closed her eyes
to everything but this golden man.

And it was marvelous. His hands traveled over her,
starting the insidious need that made her cling to
him desperately.

It was a night of love, and she woke the next morning in Oregon's arms, in the dusky light of Saturday's
dawn. She sat up and looked down at him. Long,
thick lashes shadowed his broad cheekbones, and
his bare chest rose and fell in regular rhythm.

"Oregon! You have to go home. Aunt Mattie will see
you." He opened his eyes and focused on her. One
corner of his mouth lifted in a crooked smile. "My
intentions are honorable. I want to marry you."

She tugged the sheet to her chin and tried to avoid

looking at Oregon's enticing chest or inviting mouth. She overcame the temptation to lean down and brush his lips with hers.

"Oregon, will you get up and go home?"

He chuckled and pulled her down. "Come here, darlin'. I'll go, and the world won't be scandalized."

She summoned her stiffest resolve and sat up again. "You need to go now."

"Darlin' . . ."

"Don't you start that 'darlin' ' business in your sexy voice. You know what it does to me!"

He sat up, his face inches from hers, his green eyes flashing with golden promises. He wrapped his fingers in her curls. "What does my voice do, darlin'?" Their faces were inches apart. And his words were suggestive, his mouth irresistible.

"Oh, Oregon!" And then she was in his arms, with his mouth on hers, and she never knew who made the first move. An hour later, dazed, aware of sunlight really streaming through the windows, she sat up and tried again.

"Oregon, please go home."

He chuckled and got up without argument. She watched the powerful muscles in his legs, his sleek, trim buttocks flex as he walked, and she almost called him back. Almost. He picked up the black briefs and snapped them on, then turned and caught her staring. He winked, a lusty, leering wink as he drawled, "It's all yours, darlin'."

"You are tempting, Oregon."

"Oh, darlin'." He headed toward the bed, dropping his jeans.

"Oregon, get dressed!"

With a grin he reversed direction and stepped into his pants. And she happily returned to watching him. He was fascinating. The muscles in his back rippled as he sucked in his flat stomach and zipped his jeans, buttoned the waistband, then bent down to pick up the brown leather belt and slide it around his lean hips. Once again she marveled at the width of his shoulders in relation to the narrowness of his waist and hips. As he shrugged into his shirt, he smiled, asking with innocence, "Aren't you getting dressed, darlin'?"

"Yes, after you're gone and it's safe."

"Safe? There's something dangerous about me?"

"Everything is dangerous about you!"

He grinned. "That's good. I'd hate to be safe." He crossed the room and dropped a kiss on her forehead, looked into her eyes, and then sat down to pull her into his arms and really kiss her.

His tongue met hers, confirmed what they had found before, demanded more, and gave delight before he released her. "Darlin', think about a wedding date. Soon."

"Oregon, I don't know you. A week ago I didn't know you existed."

"That so? Well, we'll take care of the little details, getting to know me, the paper, Mattie. Charity, marry me and we'll live just yards away from her. And the landscape business—how much are the debts, hon?"

"I won't let you get involved." She raised her chin, and he grinned as he rose to his feet.

"What time does Ziza arrive?"

"Late this afternoon. Oregon, don't misunderstand, but I'd . . ." She hesitated. It was difficult to put her feelings into words.

He quirked an eyebrow questioningly. "What is it, hon?"

"Well, Ziza tends to take over, and—I guess it's a

nang-up from childhood, but she makes me ner-
ous." She looked out the window. "Money means
nore to her than men. And my father didn't make a
ot of money. She wasn't happy to have me live with
ner."

"Charity, that's over now. Let it go," he said force-
ully.

She met his solemn gaze and continued. "By three
'll probably have a headache."

"If you weren't that close, why's she coming to see
ou? Is Mattie important to her?"

Charity took a deep breath and tried to keep her
voice level, unaware of Oregon's gaze dropping to the
sheet as she clenched it in her fists. "No, they hardly
know each other. They're on opposite sides of the
amily. She's coming because I inherited some of
Uncle Hubert's money and I'll inherit everything
when Aunt Mattie . . . later. I'll be worth noticing
hen."

"Well, hell's bells. Send her packing."

"No, she's my aunt. That's something else. She
aught me to never call her aunt or acknowledge the
relationship. She had a date with a college guy once
and made me double-date with his little brother, and
wasn't supposed to tell that she was over twenty-
ive."

Oregon swore softly. Ignoring him, she added,
"She's my mother's sister. I can't be unkind, but I
dread her visit. As I said, I'll probably get a headache.
Oregon, I don't want her to know you've proposed,
and it really would be easier if you weren't here. She's
very forceful."

"How long since you've seen her?"

"It's been a long time. I was in high school."

"You might not get a headache now," he said dryly.

"You've probably changed a lot since then. And I'm not worried about forceful women."

Suddenly she felt better and grinned at him. "I'll bet not. You know you can turn them to putty."

"Putty, huh? Maybe I should stay a little longer. . . ."

"Oregon!"

"I'm going. Some putty!"

"You don't know this one!"

He leaned down, placing his hands on her shoulders and looking into her eyes. "Darlin', this is the fourteenth of May. Let's have a May wedding."

"Oregon, I don't know you that well!"

"You know me better than you do any other man on earth," he said with a smugness that aggravated her and made her blush.

"Let me make up my mind without interference, Oregon!"

"Darlin', you made up your mind a while back, whether you want to admit it or not." He winked, then opened her screen window.

"Talk about forceful people . . ."

He grinned. "This is different, and you know it."

"Suppose Aunt Mattie sees you leave?"

"It won't matter. I'll be part of the family soon. She'll think I'm in the yard looking for Billy."

"Billy! Dammit, Oregon, I can't live with that goat!"

Oregon's grin widened, the dimples punctuating it. "Darlin', I'll take you over a goat any day. Billy can live on the farm. Now, get dressed and I'll think about you, think about you getting out of bed, in a tub of hot, sudsy water . . ." He spoke in Rory Runyon's intimate, husky drawl, and she burned.

"Oregon, go!"

He grinned, waved, and stepped through the window to the patio. Flopping back onto the pillow she gazed dreamily out the window and watched Oregon stroll across the yard as if he owned it. Sometimes he acted as if he owned the world. And then there were moments . . . She remembered how vulnerable and solemn he had sounded when he'd said, "This wasn't something taken lightly . . ." Did Oregon really need her as badly as he indicated? He wanted to marry her! Oregon Brown/Rory Runyon had proposed! The idea made her tingle like a reverberating bell. Marriage! Did she need to get to know him better? Wisdom said yes and her heart screamed no. She would try to listen to wisdom today.

And today Ziza would arrive. Ziza. "Oh, lordy," she breathed aloud, and threw back the covers.

Just before noon, after fixing Aunt Mattie's breakfast and finishing the housecleaning, Charity studied her reflection in the dresser mirror, smoothed the straps of her white sundress, then glanced around the room. Her gaze drifted to the bed, and in her mind she could clearly see Oregon's big, golden body stretched out on it, remember how he had kissed her as no other man had . . .

She burned with the memory, and tingled and ached. "Dammit, Oregon! Get out of my mind."

The doorbell rang. With a lift of her chin, Charity walked grimly down the hall. Her palms felt damp, her nerves strained, and her cheeks were burning as she flung open the door. Determined to present a positive, relaxed front, she exclaimed, "Come in! Come—"

Oregon grinned and stepped forward to take her into his arms. "Thanks, darlin'. It's good to be here." He leaned down to kiss her.

"Oregon!" She wriggled away and glared at him. "What are you doing here?"

He extended a bouquet of red roses and white carnations. "I thought you might like some flowers for the festive occasion."

"Thank you. They're beautiful."

"You sound as if I'd presented you with a bundle of weeds."

"These will be a red flag under Ziza's nose. She'll have a thousand questions about who sent them and why."

"Want me to throw them out?"

"No!" She smelled them. "They're lovely. I'll put them in the living room."

"Good."

Acutely aware of Oregon's watchful eyes, she placed them on a table. She wished he would go. It made her nervous to think about facing Ziza with Oregon present. She straightened and saw Oregon settle on the sofa.

"Oregon, I'm expecting Ziza any time now."

"Yeah, I know."

She hated to ask him to leave, but she didn't want him to stay. They stared at each other while the seconds ticked past and then, outside, she heard a car motor grow louder and louder.

"Here she is. Oregon, you're going to complicate things," she said as she started toward the door. He followed and stood on the porch beside her.

"She might as well get to know me. I intend to be around for a long time."

How could she stay angry after that? She watched the sleek black Lincoln Continental whip into the drive. Oregon asked lightly, "You have a headache?"

"No, I don't." She met a satisfied gaze.

"I didn't think you would."

A scream interrupted their conversation and a woman jumped out of the car and, arms outstretched, rushed toward them. "Charity!"

Eleven

"She's the age your mother would have been?"
Oregon asked softly, and Charity knew why. Ziza was
slim, carefully fed, with a figure that was exercised
and groomed for hours each day. With a wild tangle of
black curls, heavy makeup, and a simple black dress
that probably had had a staggering price tag, Ziza
Feathers hurried up the walk to them. As a handsome, brown-haired man climbed out from behind
the wheel, Oregon muttered, "My goodness, I do
believe she robbed the cradle."

The man was young; he had to be close to Charity's
age. Then Charity momentarily forgot him as Ziza
flung her arms around Charity while big blue eyes
sized up Oregon Brown.

"Charity, love! It's simply been ages. And you'll have
to introduce me right now!"

She released Charity, who said, "Ziza, this is

Mattie's neighbor, Oregon Brown. Oregon, this is Ziza."

Oregon accepted Ziza's extended hand for a brief shake. "Glad to meet you, Ziza," he said blandly.

"Oh, my goodness. That delectable voice! You just have to be the man I talked to on the phone."

Charity felt as if she had stepped back into quicksand. Why hadn't Oregon let sleeping dogs lie and stayed home?

"I'm the very one."

"And you have a date with Charity tonight . . ."

"That's right."

At the foot of the porch steps the tall, slender man paused. Charity glanced at him. He was handsome, with blue eyes and brown, wavy hair, but he couldn't be a day over twenty-six, which made Ziza twice his age.

She clasped Charity and Oregon by the arms. "Well, you two will meet Rolf anyway. Bernard, my precious Bernard, got sick in Dallas and flew home, and Rolf came down to drive me back so I wouldn't have to travel alone. Isn't that the sweetest thing!" As if on cue, in a scene that had been rehearsed a hundred times, she turned. "Rolf, darling, come here and meet these nice people."

He climbed the steps, his blue eyes fastened on Charity as if she were a long-sought-after gem, and suddenly Charity knew it wasn't simply a matter of Bernard's becoming ill. Ziza had planned this just as surely as there was a sun in the sky. Ziza linked her arm through Rolf's. "This, darlings, is Rolf Feathers. Rolf, here's Charity Jane . . ."

Rolf picked up her hand, holding it too long between his, while his eyes seemed to devour her. "I've heard so much about you, Charity."

"And this is her neighbor, Oregon Brown," Ziza continued happily.

Reluctantly Rolf pulled his gaze from Charity and shook hands briefly with Oregon.

"Now, where's Mattie? Let's go inside." Ziza linked her arm through Oregon's, gazing up at him with wide eyes, while Rolf took Charity's arm. And Charity knew absolutely that Ziza was up to one of her games.

Oregon held the door, shifting his arm to take Ziza's. In his coaxing, melting baritone, he said, "Ziza, you greet Mattie. I'll be right along." And he winked at Ziza.

For just an instant Ziza looked startled, then she smiled and sailed inside. Oregon looked the soul of innocence as he turned to Charity and Rolf.

"Charity, I want to show Rolf the flowers." Oregon motioned with a jerk of his head. "Come here, Rolf."

Oregon looked guileless, but Charity had a feeling she was throwing Rolf to the wolves. Since when was Oregon interested in flowers? There wasn't so much as a dandelion blooming in his yard. And he couldn't be interested in Rolf either. Oregon led Rolf away, and Charity went inside. She found Ziza in the living room.

"Where is everyone?"

"Aunt Mattie," Charity called, "Ziza's here." She turned to her aunt. "Ziza, why did you bring Rolf?"

"I told you, sweetie, to drive me home." She winked. "Besides, Charity, it will do you good to throw a little jealousy into Oregon Brown. Charity, that man is a hunk! I wouldn't have guessed. He is luscious, and what a voice! When you said you had a date, I could just imagine some sweet little college boy, not Mr. Muscle. And dimples too!" Her blue eyes drifted over Charity. "You've grown up."

"That happens," Charity murmured, her thoughts elsewhere. What was Oregon doing? *Showing the flowers to Rolf?*

Ziza continued blithely. "Well, Rolf will give him some competition. It never hurts, Charity. Take it from someone who knows. Darling, if you need any help with investments—I know you'll inherit the— Mattie! It's so nice to see you again."

Ziza kissed Mattie's cheek, and they sat down while Ziza explained Bernard's absence and Rolf's presence. Then she announced, "Now, I'm taking us all to dinner tonight. No arguments. I know you and Oregon Brown have a date, Charity, but you can run along after dinner."

Charity grimaced inwardly. Ziza hadn't been there half an hour and things were in an uproar, plans were changed, and the rest of the day and night were looking grim. Then Rolf and Oregon appeared, and Charity straightened in shock. Rolf looked ashen beneath his tan, while Oregon was smiling innocently as he settled in a chair near hers. Ziza's eyes narrowed, constantly darting back and forth between the two men, while she introduced Rolf to Mattie.

Mattie smiled. "How nice of you to drive Ziza to Enid."

Rolf shifted nervously, shooting one quick glance at Oregon. "I'm glad . . ." His voice cracked. He swallowed and tried again. "I'm glad to do it." Then, almost as an afterthought, he said. "When we get to Oklahoma City, I want Ziza to meet the woman I'm in love with."

It was Ziza's turn to look startled. "Silly thing! He's joking." She cast steely eyes on Rolf. "You know you told me there's no woman in your life right now."

"I forgot about her."

All eyes in the room focused on Rolf, and he giggled nervously. "Just a joke," he muttered.

Charity looked intently at Oregon. He looked too, too pleased. His gaze shifted to hers, and, as if he saw the question in her eyes, he shrugged one broad shoulder.

Undaunted, Ziza wriggled in her chair, zeroed in on Charity and Oregon, and said, "Darlings, I just have to know how you two met."

"Over the fence, you might say," Charity replied. "We're neighbors."

"And what is your line of work, Oregon?"

Charity waited to see what he would say. Oregon smiled, placing one booted ankle on his knee and resting a hand on it. "I'm a disc jockey."

Ziza frowned. Charity knew that each of Ziza's past seven husbands had had more than average-sized bank accounts. She looked at Oregon's happy smile and realized he knew exactly what he was doing.

"A disc jockey." Ziza pronounced it like a death sentence. "Well, of course, Mattie now owns the paper here. Even though dear Hubert is gone, I'm sure you can find a nice job at the paper. Something with a little more future in it."

"Oh, I like being a DJ. I enjoy my days at home. Just Billy and me. My kid, Billy." He gave Ziza another dimpled smile, and Charity left it alone. She wasn't going to explain Billy either. Oregon continued cheerfully, "I can stretch out in my hammock while Billy frolics in the yard."

Ziza looked stricken. Mattie unknowingly added fuel to the blaze. "Oh, Ziza, Billy is so cute. That's how Oregon and Charity met. That naughty little Billy came through the fence and ruined some of Charity's plants."

"Kids will be kids," Oregon said with a smile.

Ziza glanced at Charity. "Sweetie, I need to freshen up. Will you show me the way?"

Charity rose and walked down the hall. Before they reached the bathroom, Ziza took her arm and pulled her into a bedroom, closing the door after them.

"My dear, I didn't come a moment too soon." She shivered. "That man is gorgeous! He's a hunk and so-o-o sexy, but, sweetie, he's not the man for you. I mean it, dearie. Don't get tied up with a divorced man who won't work, who has no ambition. He wants to stay home and play with his kid. There's no future in that!"

"Well, Ziza, I'll have to make up my own mind."

"Sweetie, looks aren't everything. A disc jockey who doesn't want to work during the day!"

"That's the same reaction I had when I met him. About working during the day. The disc jockey part is just fine."

"Oh, my God. Charity, I don't know what happened to Rolf. You don't suppose that Brown punched him one, do you?"

"Oregon? Rolf doesn't have any bruises that show."

"No, but he's acted damned strange since he stayed outside to look at the flowers. There's no woman in his life. Sweetie, I'll see about Rolf. You dump Oregon and try an evening with Rolf. He's in stocks and bonds and he has a brilliant future."

"Thanks anyway, Ziza. I'll take my chances with Oregon."

"You're not serious about him, are you?"

"I am," Charity answered happily. "I'm in love with him." It felt good to say it and it sounded so right!

"Oh, my God. Oh, sweetie, you're just looking at his

gorgeous body. The man is a bum! Living out here in the sticks, too!"

"It's pretty nice here, Ziza."

"And he has Billy."

"I'll admit I don't like Billy, but if I marry Oregon, he's promised to send Billy away." Charity was beginning to enjoy herself.

Ziza's eyes widened. "Oh, my God, it gets worse! He'll get rid of his kid to have you as his wife. Charity, the man's after your money. Or Aunt Mattie's money."

"I don't think so."

"He is! Get rid of him. And for heaven's sake, give Rolf a chance. Take my advice. Rolf's a whiz with investments."

"Thanks, Ziza. Shall we go back?"

"I hope you do what I say. You're just like your mother, looking at the world with wide-eyed innocence. The first handsome devil to throw the charm at you, and you fall for him. A gorgeous body and sexy voice are fine, but money is what counts! Now, you take your aunt's advice—give Rolf a chance. Dear, his future is marvelous. Get rid of this lazy Oregon bum!"

"He's not really a bum!" Charity laughed, while Ziza's brow furrowed in a frown.

"Charity, I see my duty. I want you to come back to Kansas City with me."

Charity felt a knot tighten in her stomach. "I can't leave Mattie. There are a thousand things to do here, but thanks." Charity smiled and relaxed. Ziza wasn't as formidable as she remembered. Or time had changed her reaction to her aunt. "Shall we go back to the living room?"

Ziza stared at her. "You know, you have grown up."

"It's been a long time," Charity said gently. The

past was over and done. And some old hurts were laid to rest. Without waiting for Ziza, Charity turned away. Ziza caught up with her, and together they returned to the living room.

To a silent living room. Mattie was rocking gently, Oregon was gazing out the front window with a smile on his face, and Rolf looked as if he were sitting on a tack. The moment they entered, Ziza said, "I told Charity and Mattie, and now I'll tell you boys: I'm taking everyone to dinner tonight." Her gaze rested on Oregon. "No arguments. I know you two have a date, but you can put it off one night. I haven't seen Charity in years." She turned to face Mattie. "I was just telling Charity, I want you to come home with me, both of you." She rummaged in her purse for a cigarette, and placed it between her lips. "It would be so nice to have you for a week."

"Thank you, Ziza," Aunt Mattie began.

Suddenly Oregon leaned forward with a lighter in his hand, holding it for Ziza. Charity stared at him in amazement. She hadn't seen him smoke one cigarette. Ziza leaned forward, inhaled, and, while she was close to Oregon, looked up into his eyes. Her full dark lips curved in a tempting smile. Oregon smiled in return as she said a throaty, "Thank you, Oregon." She straightened and waved her cigarette in the air, not allowing Aunt Mattie to continue.

"Don't say it, Mattie. Don't decline yet. You and Charity think it over."

"That's nice, Ziza," Mattie replied. "Charity can go, but I don't travel so well any longer."

"I could put you two on a plane! Mattie, you'd love it." And suddenly Charity's sinking feeling returned. Ziza knew where the defenses were down. To get

Charity away from Oregon, Ziza would work on Mattie.

"Ziza." Oregon cut in in a husky baritone that stopped Ziza's chatter instantly. "I can't wait any longer. I want to have a little chat with you about Charity." Charity closed her eyes briefly, merciful blackness shutting out everyone. What was he up to now? Oregon didn't know Ziza. "The rest of you will excuse us, won't you?" While he spoke lightly, his gaze rested on Rolf, who paled visibly. What had Oregon done to the man? As Oregon took Ziza's arm, Charity wondered if Ziza had met her match. Or vice-versa. Ziza could twist most men around her finger with ease.

As soon as Oregon and Ziza were out of sight, Aunt Mattie sat forward, her gnarled fingers gripping the arms of the rocker. "You two sit and talk while I get us some tea."

"Let me do it, Aunt Mattie." Charity jumped up and went to the kitchen. She was in time to see Oregon stroll across the yard with his arm across Ziza's shoulders. Beneath the shade of the elm he turned Ziza to face him. He looked relaxed, his hands slipping into his back pockets while he talked. Ziza seemed to draw herself up, and Charity wondered what Oregon was saying. Whatever he had said to Rolf had finished the man off. She couldn't imagine anything that would faze Ziza. Charity carried a tray of glasses of iced tea back to the living room. She offered one to Mattie, then one to Rolf, who shot her a quizzical glance, snatched a glass, and quickly mumbled his thanks.

"What business are you in, Rolf?" she asked.

"Investments," he said shortly, and turned to

Mattie. "That's an interesting painting over the mantel."

Mattie thanked him, and they launched into a discussion of the picture and of how Mattie and Hubert had bought it in Oklahoma City. Charity glanced at the print of Gainsborough's *Blue Boy*. Rolf had surely seen it a dozen times before. What had Oregon done to him? She studied him openly. There wasn't a mark on him.

As if aware of her observation, he flicked a nervous glance at her, then back to the picture. He rose and moved to sit by Mattie, across the room from Charity. Oh, Oregon had done something, all right!

And then she heard Oregon's voice, his marvelous baritone, talking about the weather and the Plaza in Kansas City. Ziza and Oregon entered the room. Spots of color marked Ziza's cheeks, and her blue eyes were flinty. Oregon looked relaxed and happy as a lark.

And within ten minutes Charity realized that Oregon, Mattie, and she were carrying the conversation. Ziza and Rolf sat in grim silence until Ziza suddenly rose to her feet. "Charity, Mattie, I'm dreadfully sorry, but suddenly I feel ill. I think we'll be on our way to Oklahoma City now so I can take a plane home if I get worse."

Everyone rose and drifted to the door, while Mattie offered to let them stay at her house. As Ziza put her arms around Charity to hug her farewell, she whispered, "Keep in touch. I wish you all the happiness in the world."

Charity wondered what had brought that on. Ziza rushed to the car and climbed in beside Rolf. They waved good-bye as the black car drove out of sight.

"I'm so sorry Ziza became ill," Mattie said. "It's a

shame, when you haven't seen each other for so many years. Ziza's always tied up in her own interests, though. She should've come to see you those years when you were in high school."

Charity put her arm around Mattie's thin shoulders. "I had you and Uncle Hubert, and that was better."

"You're a sweet girl, Charity," Aunt Mattie said, and if she had left it at that, Charity would have felt a warm glow, but Mattie went right on. "Don't you think so, Oregon?"

"She's sweet as chocolate candy." He winked at Charity, and she blushed.

"Hubert and I were so worried about raising a young girl, and that prom night you stayed out until five A.M., Charity, you'll never know what that did to your uncle!"

"That was a long time ago," Charity said emphatically to Oregon.

With one of his smug smiles that made her feel as if a slow-burning fuse had been ignited beneath her feet, he said, "Oh, yes, the time when Jack Mullins ran out of gas."

Charity wanted to explode. Was there anything Mattie and Hubert hadn't told Oregon? "My, what a memory you have about things that don't concern you!" she snapped, and his dimples appeared.

"If you two will excuse me," Mattie said, "I think I need a little nap."

Oregon held the door for Charity and Mattie, then followed them inside. Charity began picking up glasses and napkins while Mattie went into her bedroom. Oregon, with glasses in each hand, followed Charity into the sunny kitchen. She set down the tray and turned to face him.

"All right. What did you do to them?"

His brows arched. "Who, me?"

"Come on, Oregon. I've never seen Ziza like that in my life."

He grinned, his green eyes as devilish as that old goat of his. "You have to fight fire with fire, and all that. She resorted to dirty tricks to get you separated from me for a week and I couldn't let her get away with it." He hooked his thumbs in his belt. "If Mattie wants to go to Kansas City, you and I will take her this summer."

As aggravated and curious as Charity was, she was also thrilled by his words. But she wasn't going to let it drop. "You aren't off the hook. What did you do?"

"Hon, you said Ziza understands money, and she's easy to handle." He looked down at her with a heavy-lidded gaze. "She's not an independent woman. She's easy to manipulate, whereas you, darlin', are like moving the Rock of Gibraltar."

"Oregon, that's ridiculous! It's the other way around. Ziza? Easy to handle?"

"Sure. You were holding your own just fine. I simply speeded things up for you." A very steely note came into his voice. It was a tone she had heard only once, when he had waited in the yard the night before and told her to come outside. "I just explained to her that she mustn't interfere in your life or mine."

"That's all?"

"Well, I told her my finances were sufficient to support you comfortably."

"You must have been very convincing." She was beginning to get the drift of the conversation she had witnessed beneath the elm.

"I have my persuasive moments." He pulled his thumbs out of his belt and reached for her. "Come here." He leaned close and whispered, "Darlin', I hope to hell to get my way. I want you, Charity Jane, and I'm going to fight for all I'm worth . . ."

Her pulse was drumming so loudly she couldn't hear the rest of his words. She gazed into his hungry eyes. "I'm like the Rock of Gibraltar? Really, Oregon, when it comes to you, I'm mush. Soppy, gooey mush."

"You don't say!" he replied, and kissed her.

She returned the kiss, wrapping her arms around his neck and clinging to him until he raised his head. "Charity, I did run them off. Are you sorry?"

She shook her head. "Not really. Ziza never did care about me. I was a nuisance."

"Darlin', forget that time. I wish I could wipe that year out of your life, but it's over and gone."

"I know. It doesn't matter now. Life improved when I came to live with Aunt Mattie and Uncle Hubert. They were good to me, and I loved them, but then, I guess you know all about that. Oregon, have they told you everything about me?"

"Everything!" he said with a wide grin.

"I hope you're wrong! Do you smoke?"

"Nope. Don't smoke, don't chew tobacco . . ."

"Why do you carry a lighter?"

"Oh. I thought Ziza might smoke. Sometimes it's handy to have a lighter."

"And what did you do to Rolf? Did you hit him?"

"Hit him?" His green eyes gazed guilelessly at her. "Darlin', I wouldn't just up and hit a man. I showed him Mattie's roses."

"Oregon . . ."

"Well, maybe I said a few things, but I didn't hit him. I told him I belonged to the Enid Mafia . . ."

"The Enid Mafia! Oh, dammit, Oregon."

". . . and if he so much as looked at you, I'd put out a contract on him."

"That's ridiculous and terrible!"

"I don't like competition for my girl."

She couldn't help but smile. He kissed her temple, murmuring softly, "Charity, have you reached a decision yet?"

"I can't be like Ziza. I can't rush into marriage when I don't know you."

"It isn't time that's important. Don't you feel something special?"

"Yes. But I still won't rush into a lifetime commitment."

He moved away. "I'll be back in a little while."

"All right, Oregon." He had yielded too easily, and she had a suspicion he was up to something again.

"I'll just go out through the back."

She followed him to the patio. "Oregon . . ." He paused at the door. "Thanks. Ziza isn't really that fond of me."

She expected one of his light, quick replies, but instead he turned back to her and cupped her face in his hands. "Darlin', you'll get to know me. I can wait a little. But, Charity, you'll never be another Ziza, and I'm going to be your one and only as long as I draw breath."

She trembled and wrapped her arms around him, standing on tiptoe to kiss him. Finally she pulled away and said shakily, "How can I keep my wits about me when you say things like that?"

"There's something else. If I buy the paper, I'll have to go to work during the day."

"That's all right," she answered. "I'll have to work during the day too."

"Not necessarily. I know, don't protest. I can see it

coming in your blue eyes. Darlin', if I work during the day, I want the nights with you. I'll retire Rory Runyon."

She smiled, her full lips curving sweetly as she trailed her fingers along his cheek. "I won't mind, because I'll have Rory Runyon all to myself. I went through agony while you talked to Samantha."

"Samantha? Oh, on the program."

For a long moment they gazed into each other's eyes, wordless messages passing between them, confirmation, desire. Oregon turned abruptly. "I'll be back in a little while."

And he was. As Charity peeled a potato for Mattie's dinner, she looked out the kitchen window and saw Oregon step out from behind the crepe myrtle. She saw his hair, his eyes, and his long legs, but between eyes and legs he was hidden behind an armload of boxes and books.

She hurried to get the potato on to boil, rinsed her hands, and rushed to the back door as Oregon called, "Charity!"

"What on earth?" she asked when she stepped outside.

"Have you got a minute?" He put everything down in a chair and straightened.

"Sure. Until I get ready for an important dinner date."

"Good. Come here." He took her hand and sat her down on the porch swing beside him, then pulled the chair filled with books and boxes close beside them. He put a scrapbook in her lap, opened it, and said, "Now, darlin', here's my past."

She looked down at pictures of Oregon at an early age. "Oregon, I'm glad to look at these, but this isn't what I meant about knowing you!"

He could look so damned innocent and amazed. "It isn't? Darlin', here's my whole past." He rummaged in the stack and withdrew a fat book. "Here's my baby book. You can read when I got my first tooth, when I crawled, what my first word was . . ."

"Dammit, there's more to it than that."

"How can you swear over a baby book? Come on, darlin', let's read, and pretty soon you'll know me."

"I'm getting to know you pretty well right now." She didn't know whether to laugh or swear. So she didn't do either. For the next hour she looked at Oregon's scrapbooks, photo albums, boxes of mementos his mother had saved. He gave her the lock of hair from his first haircut, and she tucked it away to keep.

Mattie joined them for a time, then left while they continued, until Oregon rose. "I have to go now. You keep them, Charity. I'll get everything later. Darlin', I'm sorry, but I have to do 'Nighttime.' We'll have several hours first."

"That's all right. I love 'Nighttime.' "

"I want to hear you say you love something else."

She smiled up at him as he leaned down to drop a kiss on her cheek. She stayed on the swing and watched as he lithely bounded over the fence. She was tempted to tell Mattie about his proposal, but it sounded ridiculous to think about marrying him when she had known him such a short time. She looked at the album spread open on her lap, at snapshots of a lanky young Oregon in a high-school football uniform. The cocky grin hadn't changed. But she couldn't marry someone just because she had seen all his old photos. She thumbed through a box of articles by Oregon, forgetting the time while she read. Finally she closed the box and went into the house.

Two hours later Charity was ready to go out.

Smoothing her yellow sleeveless dress, she walked to the kitchen to get Mattie's dinner on the table. As soon as it was ready she called her aunt. "Aunt Mattie, dinner."

Glancing at the clock, she saw it was five minutes until Oregon was due. Her pulse hummed along eagerly, and she felt trembly with anticipation. "Aunt Mattie," she called again.

When she didn't get an answer, she decided her aunt had taken off her hearing aid. She went to Mattie's room, but it was empty. Puzzled, she tried the bathroom. One by one, she went through each room in the house, only to find them all empty. When the doorbell rang, she opened it swiftly and faced Oregon.

One hand was resting on his waist, pushing his gray coat back and revealing a white shirt above charcoal slacks. His gaze heated her as it drifted down over her yellow dress, down to her yellow pumps, and up again. And she did the same thing in return to Oregon, her heart beating rapidly as she drank in the sight of him. How handsome he looked! Their eyes met, and she wanted to step into his arms—until she remembered Mattie.

"Have you seen Aunt Mattie?" she asked.

"No. I can't see anyone except a gorgeous curly-haired blonde. Y-u-m, yum!" He reached for her, but she sidestepped him and held his hands.

"Oregon, I can't find Aunt Mattie. Come in and let me call the neighbors."

Oregon followed her into the kitchen and lounged casually against the door, looking so disturbing, marvelous, and distracting that she finally turned her back on him while she discussed Mattie's whereabouts with the neighbors.

In fifteen minutes Charity was frantic. She hung up the phone after talking to the last person on Mattie's phone list. "No one has seen her. Where can she be?"

He crossed the room and put his hands on her shoulders. "Now, don't worry. Enid's a pretty safe place to wander around in, and sometimes she just likes to take a walk. She's done this before, and I've helped Hubert find her. I'll call the police—I know someone down there—and just alert them. Then you and I'll look around the neighborhood."

After he made the call, they climbed into separate cars to drive in opposite directions, agreeing to meet again in thirty minutes. When they met after half an hour, Charity waited nervously while Oregon parked and climbed into the car beside her. "I haven't seen her, but Billy's gone," he said.

"She took Billy with her?"

"I think so. He hás a leash that usually hangs on the back porch. It's gone and the gate was closed."

"I feel a little better to think that goat might be with her. I'll look some more. Where can she be?"

"I called the police and they're making an all-out effort. It's getting dark. Why don't we go together now? I'll drive."

Charity was getting so edgy, she was glad to let him. As Oregon drove, she twisted her hands together. "I can imagine so many terrible things. She isn't wearing her hearing aid, and she can't hear a car honk or the motor—"

"Charity." Pulling to the curb, he turned and cupped her face in his hands, and his voice was gentle and calm. "Don't imagine anything bad. She's with Billy. They're probably sitting somewhere while he chews up the flowers. Now, come on, don't worry until you have to."

"I'll try," she said grimly. "This is why I can't leave her alone. I don't know what I'll do, Oregon. I can't take her to Tulsa to live with me and I can't move in with her and give up my life."

A strange look flickered over his face, one almost of pain. In a deep, solemn voice that sounded so vulnerable, he said, "Darlin', I've asked you to marry me. Isn't that in your choices?"

"Of course it is! I was talking about the immediate future."

"So am I."

"I'll still have to figure out what to do about Mattie. She can't live alone."

"Hon, you'll work it out, but remember, this happened while you were living with her."

"That just makes me feel worse."

"No. What I'm trying to tell you is that there is just so much you can do and no more. Hon, when we're married, we'll live by her and you can hire a companion for her, someone to stay all the time. We'll talk about it later. Let's try the park by the zoo." He backed the car down the driveway.

"That's miles away!"

"Not impossible, though."

They found Mattie sitting in the park, just as Oregon had guessed. Billy was tethered nearby, chomping on grass beneath one of the tall yellow lights that shed a glow over the entire park. Charity was so relieved she could scarcely speak, but Mattie seemed to feel nothing was wrong. She simply remarked on what a nice stroll she and Billy had had.

By the time Oregon and Charity had gotten Mattie home and called the police and neighbors, only an hour remained before Oregon had to go to the station. So Charity grilled hamburgers, they ate with Mattie, and then Charity walked to the door to say good-bye to Oregon.

After a long, heated kiss, Oregon gazed down at her. "I'll tell Bob to hold the line for your requests. No one will get through except you."

"Can you do that?"

"Sure." He grinned. "Have any big requests like 'I've Never Been a Woman Before'?"

She blushed and was grateful they stood on the darkened porch. "Enough from you! I didn't think you'd remember."

"I can tell you exactly. 'The Men in My Life,' 'Touch—' "

"Now, stop! Did you play any of those pieces particularly for me?"

"Don't tell me you didn't know!"

"Well, how could I be sure?"

His voice shifted down to the low hum of an idling motor. "When I kiss you like this and then play 'You Do Something to Me'—hon, it's only for you!" He pulled her to him and kissed her in such a manner that Charity's system underwent a major upheaval. When Oregon released her, she stood in his arms, dazed, gazing up at him with wide, befuddled eyes. And she almost lost her wits and threw over the traces, almost cast aside her long-standing, firm promises to herself not to rush into marriage. She almost said yes. "Oregon . . ."

His eyes narrowed, and he waited. And while he waited, Charity's wits settled down, like a bird on a branch, from the flight caused by his kiss. Settled down enough that she said simply, "I'll listen to 'Nighttime.' "

"Something tells me that wasn't what you started to say."

"Just give me a little time. T-i-m-e!"

"I am. Want to go to church with me tomorrow? I'll take Mattie, too."

"Oregon, I mean, give me months' of time."

"Months, huh?"

She didn't like the way he said that word. "You're going to be late for the show."

" 'Night, darlin'." He hurried down the walk.

In a daze Charity undressed for bed and settled down to listen to "Nighttime." The music filled the darkened bedroom, and then Oregon's voice came on, husky, sexier than ever.

"Hi, darlin'. Here's 'Nighttime,' on station KKZF. This is Rory Craig Runyon, darlin', I'll be playing some night songs"—his voice lowered, sliding down the scale to another octave—"night songs only for you."

Charity felt on fire. "Darlin', it's a gorgeous night, a night for love. My empty arms need you, want you. Here's a song for you: 'Black Satin Sheets.' "

Charity felt sure she must be glowing in the dark like the radio dial. Thank goodness she was alone! She hadn't heard the instrumental song before, the scratches on the record and the style of music made her think it was old, but the message was clearly Oregon Brown's! If she married Oregon—if! If they married, what would she do about Mattie?

Married to Oregon. The thought almost levitated Charity off the bed. She could picture Oregon down to the smallest detail, his big fingers on the records, his lively green-gold eyes, his charcoal slacks molding muscular legs . . .

The music ended and his voice lazed into the room,

as tantalizing as his presence. "Darlin', that's for you. Now here's something else—Captain Nemo's Fudge Bars. Fudge as te-empting and dee-licious"—his voice dropped again—"as your . . ." Pause. A pause that put Charity's whole system on hold. What was he about to say? Her imagination was the only thing that functioned, and it worked furiously. "Oh, no, Oregon," she whispered to the empty room, squeezing her eyes closed and bracing herself for the rest of his sentence.

It came in syrupy tones. ". . . as your momma made."

Charity felt as if she had just narrowly escaped getting run down by a truck. Maybe she should turn 'Nighttime' off and save her heart considerable strain. But, then again, it would be under a strain if she couldn't hear Oregon. Suddenly, getting to know Oregon far better didn't seem half so important. And wisdom whispered, "This is the one and only!"

She sat up in bed and peered at the radio. Did she want to marry Oregon?

His voice swirled around her like sweet spring water.

"Darlin', there's a big moon out now, a million stars, a night for love, for you in my arms. Here's another song for you, darlin'," and "What Are You Doing the Rest of Your Life?" came on.

Charity smiled, leaned back in bed, closed her eyes, and thought about Oregon Brown. Charity Brown. Mrs. Oregon Brown. "Mrs. Charity Brown." She said it out loud and decided it had a very nice ring to it. She didn't have any particular songs to request and tried to think of something. Her eyes flew open. She threw back the covers, rushed to the closet, turned on the lights, and pulled out her album collection. She'd send a message back to Oregon. She rummaged through the albums, selected three, turned off the lights, and settled back in bed as Oregon came over the radio.

"Did you like that one, darlin'? Let me hear from you. What song would you like? I'll play another and you call me when it's over. Here's an oldie from me to you. 'Full Moon and Empty Arms.' "

Charity listened, then dialed as soon as the music stopped. One ring, and a man answered, "KKZF 'Nighttime.' "

"This is Charity."

"Hi, Charity. Oregon said to put you through. Here goes . . ."

A ring came over the radio, and then Oregon's special voice. "Hi, there."

"Hi. This is Charity."

"Darlin', I've been waiting for your call."

She curled her toes and wished he were with her. He asked, "What do you want to request?"

" 'I Honestly Love You,' " she said.

" 'I Honestly Love You.' Sure, darlin'. Hang on while I put the record on to play." Music came on, faded, and then Oregon's sexy voice burned through the line into her soul. "It's been forever since I left you. Darlin', I need you."

She thrilled to his words, and she poured out her thoughts to him. "Oregon, I've looked at the scrapbooks, but I don't know anything about the past year in your life. I don't know about two weeks ago."

"I moved back here when my Dad died. I don't want to live on the farm. He didn't either. I have someone who runs it for me. I moved into the house. I've dated first one person, then another, and they didn't mean anything to me. Charity, we can build a new house if you'd like. You don't have to move into my old house."

"It's lovely, but let's take one thing at a time. Let's worry about that much later."

"I hope not much later."

"Oregon, why me?"

His voice lowered, dropping to depths below the surface, down to a molten heat that poured out sensuously. "There's something special about you. There's a chemistry between us. You're fun."

"I just don't know you. And aren't you rushing into marriage rapidly, after avoiding it for years?"

"I've been alone, Charity. Really alone. I left home when I was eighteen to go away to school and I didn't come back here to live until my parents were gone. I've traveled, I've devoted a lot of time and energy to—"

"Now, Oregon, I know there have been women."

"Can't deny it, hon, but it never held a lot of meaning. There never has been anybody I wanted to spend the rest of my life . . ." He paused, then said, "Uh-oh, darlin', the song's going to end. Call me later, darlin'. I love you."

Then Oregon's voice came over the air, but Charity was drifting from Oregon's last words, sailing like a bird on air currents, carried higher and higher in widening circles by Oregon's, *I love you* and *There never has been anybody I wanted to spend the rest of my life* . . . The lingering recollection of his words, his sexy voice, billowed around her.

"There. 'I Honestly Love You,' darlin', for only you and my listeners. I'm so grateful to my audience. Y'all have been great, so *responsive* . . ." Oregon's voice dropped on "responsive," drawing it out, the sound sliding down Charity's spine like his big fingers.

"Hmmm," she murmured aloud, and wriggled, a smile curving her lips.

"I can't tell you how much I've liked talking to you

in the late hours on 'Nighttime.' Night time is a special time, a very special time."

Charity felt on fire. My, she wanted Oregon! She was burning with the need for his big, strong arms, his sensational kisses.

"So, to all of my loyal listeners, I want to tell you, I've fallen in love. I mean to tell you, I'm in love with the sweetest, sexiest little gal this side of the Atlantic and Pacific oceans . . ."

Charity felt as if her eyes would pop out of her head. Her body became rigid. She went cold, then hot. Her breath stopped. "No," she whispered. "Oregon, no. . . !"

She grabbed the radio and shook it. "No!" But it didn't stop the husky, golden voice.

"I'm in love. I want to get married if and when she'll have me. I need her. And, in a way, while we didn't meet through 'Nighttime,' we came to know each other better because of 'Nighttime.' You never know where love will appear. So, I want to dedicate this next song to her, to my sweet . . ."

"Oregon!" Charity shook the radio again. "Don't announce me on 'Nighttime'!" She plunked the radio on the table and snatched up the phone to dial furiously.

". . . sweet little gal. Here's 'Be Mine Tonight,' dedicated to my darlin'."

The recorded voice came through the phone. "Good evening. This is station KKZF, broadcasting to you at one thousand on your dial. If you wish to talk to someone at the station, you may leave a message at the sound of the beep. We will be open at eight o'clock in the morning. Thank you for calling KKZF." There was a shrill beep, and Charity left her message. "Oregon Brown/Rory Runyon, will you stop! Call me—"

There was a click, and Oregon's deep voice came on. "Darlin' . . ."

"Oregon Brown, that is the lowest thing you have done! Don't pressure me into marriage! Don't announce me to the world! Don't—"

"Charity."

The word was said with the same quiet, steely authority he had used outside her window and with Ziza. And it stopped her instantly. Vaguely she wondered how anyone who was as nonchalant as Oregon could suddenly become so commanding, but he managed it with amazing ease.

He sounded solemn as he said, "Charity, I get a lot of calls from women. I wanted to explain my coolness. I needed to put a stop to them. It isn't personal, it's just Rory Runyon's chatter that touches lonely hearts—Dammit, I have to put on another record. Hang on, darlin'."

She listened to Oregon come over the air again. What he'd said made sense. She could imagine the lonely women who called him. Maybe he did have a good reason to declare his love and he hadn't said her name. Part of her mind worried over his remarks while another part listened to him say, "How was that, darlin'? Here's another for you and all—"

There was a bang, a rattle, the sound of something scraping in a jarring dissonance against the microphone, and she heard Oregon snap, "What the hell—"

Another male voice cut in above the background racket. "All right, mister, don't move. You bastard! I'm gonna blow your head off. I know you're in love with my woman!"

Twelve

Charity felt as if she had been struck by lightning. She sprang up, landing on her hands and knees, glaring at the radio, as she yelled, "No, he's not! He's in love with me!"

More scuffling sounds came, then, "Don't either one of you move. Get back against the wall, and you, Runyon, get your hands over your head."

"Look, we're on the air. Let me throw the switch—"

"You ain't throwing no switch, lover boy! I know all about you and Marlene."

"I don't know Marlene."

"He doesn't!" Charity shouted, her fingers trembling as she dialed information. "Give me the number of the police station!" Charity gasped, repeating it to herself as she dialed hastily. "He's in love with me!" she told the radio.

"Enid Police Department."

"This is Charity Webster, and I'm calling for a disc jockey at station KKZF. A man is threatening to kill him."

"At station KKZF? That's been reported, and a car is en route."

"En route? Thanks." Charity hung up and dialed KKZF and got the recording, while she heard over the radio, "You and Marlene. You've been saying all that garbage to her over the radio, thinking you could fool me. Well, you can't! She left me tonight just to listen to you."

"Look, my girl's not named Marlene. Call her and ask her."

"Huh!"

"She's not!" Charity shouted, shaking the radio. "I'm his girl, Charity Webster, you monster!"

A knock sounded. "Charity, are you all right?" Mattie asked.

"I'm fine. Someone is trying to kill Oregon!"

She flung the radio on the bed and pulled on her jeans and a shirt. The door opened, and Mattie thrust her head inside. "Someone wants to kill Oregon?" She looked around. "Where is Oregon?"

"He's at the radio station. At KKZF. A man is threatening his life! I'm going—"

"Oh, Charity, that's nice of you to rush to Oregon's rescue, but let's call the police."

"I did, and they're on their way." Charity snatched up her car keys. "I'll be right back."

"Charity, you might get hurt."

"No, I won't. The man isn't mad at me."

"I'll worry about you."

"Aunt Mattie, I'm the only one who can save Oregon. I've got to go."

"Oh, dear me." Mattie wrung her hands as she followed Charity through the house to the door to the garage.

"Now, lock up and don't leave. I'll call you!"

"Oh, dear! A man with a gun. Oh, I do dislike violence! Charity, be careful and don't aggravate him. . . ."

Charity flung herself behind the wheel of the car and closed the door. While she sped out of the garage and down the driveway, she fumbled with the radio dial until she caught Oregon's voice. He sounded as calm as if he were talking to Billy.

"Mister, I don't know Marlene. Not any Marlene. I'm in love with a woman named Jane."

The man said a rude word. There was a shout in the background, a clatter, the mike squawked, and then he heard the man's voice again. "Get back or I shoot him now! He's dead if you come closer."

"Do as he says," Oregon said quietly. "There's been a misunderstanding. Let me talk to him. You guys get back."

"Damn right, get back."

Charity's palms were wet, her brow felt damp, and her heart was a roller coaster. She honked and raced across an empty intersection as the light turned green. And into the commotion on the radio came a woman's scream. "Let me in! I'm his girlfriend! Rory! Cedric, what you are doing? Are you nuts? Cedric, I love you!" The woman screamed again. Suddenly the station went off the air. Charity swore and spun the dial, then grabbed the steering wheel to turn a corner with a squeal of tires. She ran a yellow light, racing toward station KKZF.

When she turned the corner, she saw the blinking red lights of police cars. Her heart pounded against her rib cage at the sight of an ambulance and a fire truck, their red and yellow lights flashing and casting eerie reflections on the building. There wasn't anyplace to park, so she stopped beside a police car, jumped out, and ran to the door.

A uniformed policeman blocked her path. "Sorry, miss, you can't go in."

Charity felt like sobbing, as she gasped, "I have to. I can save Rory Runyon's life!"

The man gazed at her impassively. "That's what three other women have just told me. How many women are in love with that guy?"

"I don't know about that!" Charity snapped, trying to draw herself up to her full five feet three and wishing she had pulled on something besides jeans and a white shirt. "But I'm the one he's in love with!"

The policeman leaned forward. "Good for you, honey bunch! Now, if you'll just join Runyon's fan club forming over there by the parking lot, you can sympathize with the other ladies."

"You have to let me in! I can tell that maniac that Rory loves me, not Marlene!"

"Yeah, sure, but if I let you in, I'd have to let Irene and Nancy and Ginger in. Sorry, toots, no dice."

"Dammit, his life is in your hands!"

The policeman shrugged. "I'd like to know how he does it," he mumbled. "I bet you don't know what he looks like."

"I do! He has blondish-red hair."

"That's a new one! So far I have two Tom Selleck look-alikes and one Richard Gere."

"Dammit, go look at him! He's big and blondish-redheaded and owns a goat."

"No kiddin'! Owns a goat! Honey bunch, that's a good one! Nice try. A lot more original than the other three."

Charity wanted to plant her tiny fist on his big square jaw. While she fumed and felt like crying at the same time, a woman dressed in high heels and a red satin dress came rushing up the walk.

"Officer, I'm the woman Rory Runyon loves," she said in a throaty voice.

"You don't say! I'll tell you what, that Runyon is one busy man!"

Charity stepped back. Next to a red satin dress, her sneakers and jeans would have little influence. Suddenly a shot shattered the night and everyone froze.

Charity looked up at the lighted second-story windows. Had the man shot Oregon? For another ten seconds no one moved; then a woman screamed and pandemonium broke loose.

"Let me in to him," the woman in satin gasped, and tried to shoulder past the policeman, who put out an arm and blocked her.

"Sorry, lady. You can join the others over there."

"But he may be shot!"

"Probably just a shot into the air. There'd be more commotion otherwise."

Charity hoped he was right. She looked up at the windows again, at the expanse of grass between the building and the parking lot. While the woman argued with the lawman, Charity moved away toward a tall pine that stood beside the front corner of the building. She glanced around. A group of women waited in the parking lot. A television van slowed and stopped in front. Clusters of policemen stood in the front. She searched the ground until she found a brick, put it in her shoulder bag, and began to climb the pine. She reached the second floor, opposite a window, before she was discovered.

"Hey, you!"

Charity scooted closer to the window and ignored the voice below.

"Lady, you up there in the tree!"

She looked down and saw another burly policeman standing below, hands on his hips. "Who, me?"

"Get down."

"Yes, sir," she answered politely, and shifted toward the window. She picked up the brick, then held out her bag.

"Ooops! Look out!" She dropped the bag on his head.

"Hey! Dammit, get down here."

Charity gauged the distance, drew back, and lobbed the brick through the window.

Glass shattered, leaving jagged pieces, while the policeman blew a shrill whistle and started up the pine after her. She pulled off her shoe, knocked out the pieces of glass, and climbed over the sill, oblivious of the shards that cut her hands.

As her feet hit the floor, she heard the policeman yell, "Lady, you're in trouble! You're obstructing justice. Come here!"

She ran through a darkened room, then stepped into an empty hall. For an instant she was lost. Then she heard voices coming from her right. Thankful she could move quietly in her sneakers, she hurried around a corner.

Ahead the hall was filled with police with their weapons drawn. A man in a gray suit was talking on a radio while the broad-shouldered policemen stood beside him, their backs to Charity.

How would she ever get through them? She walked as quietly as possible until she heard a clatter behind her and knew the policeman had climbed through the window.

She ran, hoping to burst through the men surrounding the room where Oregon was. Behind her
the policeman yelled, "Stop her!"

A uniformed man reached out and caught her.
Instead of fighting, she looked steadily at the man in
the suit.

"I'm Rory Runyon's fiancée. If you'll let me in there,
I can save him."

The policeman who had been chasing her caught
up with them. "She climbed a tree and broke in. I
warned her to stop."

She continued to gaze at the man in the suit.
"Please, give me a chance. He doesn't know Marlene.
Maybe the man will listen to me!"

"I can't take a chance on your getting hurt."

"You're taking a chance standing out here in the
hall. Let me go in there."

No one moved for an instant, and then the man
nodded. "All right. We'll go to the door of the control
room and you can tell the guy who you are. We'll see if
he believes you." Cold, dark eyes looked into hers.
"Are you sure you want to? That's not a toy gun."

"I'm sure. Please . . ."

He held her arm and moved through the line of
policemen. They went into the small, darkened studio, then paused at the door to the control room.
Dressed in a brown shirt and brown slacks, his black
hair standing up like spikes, the man with the gun,
Cedric, was backed into a corner. He held a rifle,
aimed at Oregon. A woman, wearing a pink bathrobe,
and her brown hair in curlers, stood a few feet away,
crying loudly. Another man, Bob, Charity assumed,
was standing behind Oregon. Oregon himself was
sitting back in his chair, his feet on the floor, hands
on his hips. He was facing the gunman, his back to

the turntables. His eyes shifted to the door, and Charity saw him stiffen. "No! Get her out of here!" he yelled.

"Wait a minute!" Cedric said. "Don't move. Who's she?"

"I'm the woman he loves!" Charity said. "He loves me, not Marlene!" She looked into Oregon's green eyes. "And I love him."

Never taking his eyes off Oregon, Cedric asked, "Are you two married?"

"No, but we're going to get married," Charity answered, and Oregon's brows drew together over the bridge of his nose.

"Gonna get married, huh? Let her in here."

"No!" Oregon shouted.

The rifle lowered a fraction. "Shut up, Runyon! Let her in here. Get over there by Runyon, where I can see you!"

"Charity, don't come in here!"

Charity looked up at the man who held her arm, saw the silent question in his eyes, and nodded. He released her, and she crossed the room to Oregon.

"Thought you said her name was Jane," the gun-man snapped.

"It is," Charity answered. "Charity Jane Webster."

"And you're going to marry him, huh? You hear that, Marlene?"

Marlene burst into fresh sobs, her shoulders shaking as she buried her face in her hands.

"Can I give her the chair?" Oregon asked.

"Hell, no. You sit right there, Runyon. So you love this woman and you're going to marry her."

"That's right, if she'll have me."

"Someone get a preacher," Cedric ordered.

"Hey, now, wait—" Oregon began.

"Shut up!" The eye of the rifle wavered a fraction, then trained on Charity. She felt as if she had turned to ice. "She'll get it first, so you sit real still and tell them cops to get a preacher."

"Now, look, you can't force her to marry me!"

"He won't!" Charity gasped. "I want to, Oregon."

"You do?"

"Dammit to hell, get a preacher or you won't have her to marry!"

"Charity . . ." Oregon looked at the man with the gun. "Can I stand up and put my arm around her?"

"Sure thing. Look at that, Marlene!"

"Oh, Cedric, you imbecile!" Marlene burst into more loud sobs while Oregon rose and folded Charity against his chest. He leaned down to whisper in her ear on the side away from the gunman. "Darlin', you shouldn't have come. We can have it annulled. You don't have to marry me under force."

She looked up at him. "I want to, Oregon."

He focused intently on her. "You do?"

"Yes. I'd already decided to say yes."

"Oh, Charity . . ." He looked at Cedric. "Listen, we're going to get married, but I want her to have a pretty dress and a church wedding and her relatives—"

"You want a hole blowed in your head?"

"No."

"Then you just shut up and marry the girl. Someone better get a preacher!"

"Get a priest," Oregon said as he pulled Charity to him again. "I want you to have a church wedding," he whispered. "A dress. Mattie will want to see you get married . . ."

"Cedric, you're going to go to jail!" Marlene wailed.

"Marlene, why didn't you care what happened to

me an hour ago! Tellin' me you had to hear Rory Runyon!"

"I'm sorry, Cedie!"

"Well, in a few minutes Mr. Rory Runyon will no longer be single! He'll have a good-looking wife."

Oregon winked at Charity, and she smiled up at him.

"Where the hell is that priest?"

"Someone's gone for him," a deep voice announced from the studio.

"When did you decide to accept?" Oregon asked her.

"Tonight. Today. Yesterday. I don't know. Maybe when I saw you in the hammock!"

He grinned.

"Well, look at the lovebirds, Marlene."

"Cedie, you're a jackass! You can't force people to marry. They can get it annulled."

"We don't want it annulled," both Charity and Oregon said at once, then laughed.

"Huh! Don't give a damn what they do later. Just want you to see that the man isn't in love with you, Marlene."

"Cedric, you're the limit!"

"Here's a priest," the deep voice said loudly. "Priest coming in."

A balding priest paused at the door, taking in the occupants of the room. "I'm Father—"

"Can the idle chitchat, Father. Marry these two."

"My son—"

"We want to get married," Oregon said quietly.

Through glasses perched on his nose, the priest's brown eyes peered first at Oregon, then at Charity. "This is irregular. . . ."

"We know," Oregon said, his arm around Charity's

waist. "We'll do it again the right way, but can you marry us now?"

"Well, we need a blood test and a few formalities, you know . . ." He looked over his shoulder at the policemen standing in the doorway behind him. The man in the gray suit nodded to him. "But I suppose we can get to those later. Very well. It's highly irregular—"

"Do it, Father," Cedric said flatly. "Marlene, you better watch. In a few minutes Rory Runyon won't be single. Hey!" he shouted. "Are there TV cameras out there? Get 'em in here to take pictures. I want all of Enid to see Rory Runyon get married."

There was a flurry of movement, and then a man appeared with a camera.

"Keep that light out of my eyes," Cedric said, waving the gun a fraction. "Stand over there and get every second of the wedding on film." Marlene began to unroll her hair.

"Your names, please," the priest said.

"Charity Jane Webster."

"Oregon Oliver Brown."

And they were married beneath the glare of a television camera, the dark scope of a rifle, the tearful sobs of Marlene, and the satisfied smirk of Cedric, with the Enid police force, station KKZF employees, and the crew of Channel Three news as an audience.

"I now pronounce you man and wife," the priest declared, as the camera whirred.

In the other room someone put on a record of the "wedding march." Oregon smiled, his dimples appearing as he pulled Charity into his arms and leaned down to kiss her, to kiss her as if they were alone and there were no audience, no gun, no camera, only the two of them.

And while Oregon kissed her, she dimly heard Cedric say, "I surrender."

Pandemonium broke loose around them. There were shouts, Marlene commenced sobbing again, the cameras whirred, and someone hugged Charity and Oregon at the same time.

Oregon released her, glanced at the chaos around them, put his arm across her shoulders, and said, "Let's get out of here, Mrs. Brown."

Epilogue

Charity stood at the kitchen stove, putting a cake in the oven. Voices carried from the family room. Kevin said clearly in his high voice, "Want to see how Mom and Dad got married the first time?"

Charity frowned as Scottie Barnes asked, "How many times did they get married?"

"Two!"

She pushed the cake into the oven and straightened. Why hadn't she put that tape of their wedding away!

"They had to get married. A guy with a gun made them. Dad said he wanted to anyway."

Clamping her jaw closed, Charity started toward the family room. As she passed the door to the utility room an arm shot out and circled her waist, capturing her.

"Hey!" she said softly as Oregon pulled her into the utility room and closed the door.

"Aha, me lovely, got you now!" Above wheat jeans and a bare chest, green-gold eyes smiled at her.

She laughed and tried to wriggle away. "Oregon, let go. Kevin is about to show the video tape of our first wedding."

"So? It'll keep him occupied until the cartoons come on. And I'll keep you occupied." He pushed the lock on the door and said, "There's a soft bundle of laundry here. Come here, darlin' . . ."

His voice could still melt her into squishy jelly. She tried one more protest as he leaned down to kiss her throat. "I just don't . . . like the whole neighborhood . . . Oregon . . . to see pictures of that wedding. Why doesn't he show the church wed—" She forgot what she had intended to say. She bent her head forward while Oregon kissed the back of her neck. Before she closed her eyes she glanced out the window. Kevin's new pet, a small brown goat, was chewing happily on a blooming rose bush. For an instant Charity focused on what was happening outside. "Oregon, that goat—"

"Mmmm, you smell so nice, Charity. Charity Brown, I love you. I mean, darlin', I am head over heels in love with you," he said, his voice dropping down to that deep level that vibrated his chest and turned Charity to mush. "Darlin' . . ." He pushed her white blouse aside and kissed the curve between her neck and shoulder, his lips trailing lower, starting scalding tingles.

"Oregon, Bonzo is eating my Sunrise rose. . . ."

"Hmmm. It can't taste half so good as you, darlin'," he murmured, and swung her down on a pile of clothes.

"Oregon! I'll have to wash these again if you . . . scatter them all . . ."

"Darlin', shhh. Charity Jane, don't you like this?" His big fingers slipped beneath the blouse to cup a full breast, to ease away the white lace.

"Oregon, I love you!" she gasped, winding her arms around his neck, threading her fingers in his soft red-gold hair.

"That's good to hear, darlin'," he murmured. "I love you and I'm going to kiss you until you stop talking to me about weddings and goats and roses. Until you melt and whimper and moan and want me, if it takes all day and all nii-aight."

And each word dropped down on her like scorching oil, oozing over her trembling nerves, burning into her like fire until he reached the word "night," said in his most adorable drawl. And Oregon Brown's two-syllable *nii-aight* wrapped around Charity's heart.

With that last word, all Charity Jane Webster Brown's attention flew into a rosy sky and was burned into oblivion by a red-gold sun called Oregon Oliver Brown.

THE EDITOR'S CORNER

There is a very special treat in store for you next month from Bantam Books. Although not a LOVESWEPT, I simply must tell you about Celeste DeBlasis's magnificent hardcover novel **WILD SWAN**. Celeste has demonstrated to us all what a superb storyteller and gifted writer she is in such works as **THE PROUD BREED** and **THE TIGER'S WOMAN**. So, you can imagine with what relish I approached the reading of the galleys of her latest novel one weekend not too long ago. I couldn't put **WILD SWAN** down. I wrapped myself in this touching, exciting, involving story and was darned sorry when I'd finished that last paragraph. I'll bet you, too, will find this epic tale riveting. Spanning decades and sweeping from England's West Country during the years of the Napoleonic Wars to the beautiful but trouble-shadowed countryside of Maryland, **WILD SWAN** is a fascinating story centered around an unforgettable heroine, Alexandria Thiane. And the very heart of the work is an exploration of love in its many facets—passionate, enduring, transcendent. **WILD SWAN** is a grand story, by a grand writer. Do remember to ask your bookseller for this novel; I really don't think you'll want to wait until it comes out in paperback!

And now to the LOVESWEPTS you can look forward to reading next month.

In **TOUCH THE HORIZON** (LOVESWEPT #59) Iris Johansen gives us the tender story of Billie Callahan, the touching young madcap introduced last month in **CAPTURE THE RAINBOW.** On her own at last in the mysterious desert land of Sedikhan, Billie is driving her jeep toward a walled city when she is rescued from a terrifying sandstorm by a dashing figure on a black stallion. He sweeps her into his arms and steals

(continued)

her heart. Shades of the Arabian Nights! Those of you who've read many of Iris's books in the past will recognize some old friends and thrill to the golden-haired, blue-eyed hero whose kisses send Billie spinning off the edge of the world. This lively adventure tale may be Iris's most wonderful love story to date! Don't be too frustrated now that I haven't given you the hero's name. It's a surprise from Iris. And do let me tantalize you with just a few words: he's a poignant character introduced in an early work and through letters I know many of you have complimented Iris on his creation, rooted for him, taken him into your hearts. At the end of Chapter One, you'll know his name and, I suspect, you'll be cheering!

One of the pleasures of publishing LOVESWEPT romances is discovering talented new writers, wonderful storytellers who bring us their unique insights into the special relationships between men and women. This month we're introducing two of our most exciting new discoveries: first, BJ James, whose novel **WHEN YOU SPEAK LOVE** (LOVESWEPT #60) offers an intense, dramatic and touching romance with a truly endearing cast of characters. While it was heartbreaking tragedy that brought Jake Caldwell and Kelly O'Brian together, what followed was the nurturing of a special kind of love between two people who've longed for closeness but have never known its intimate joy. We think you'll agree that BJ's first novel for LOVESWEPT is beautifully and sensitively written, a truly memorable debut.

Our second "debutante" brings a delicious sense of humor to her first LOVESWEPT romance. Joan Elliott Pickart may be **BREAKING ALL THE RULES** (LOVE-SWEPT #61) in this irresistible confection, but you'll be delighted to join in the fun! Blaze Holland and Taylor Shay both vowed they weren't looking to fall in love that wintry day in New York City, but the stormy weather wasn't the only thing beyond their control. Blaze is one of the most unforgettable heroines we've seen in a long time—and Taylor the perfect foil for her headlong tumble into the arms of love. These two give a new romantic flavor to the notion of popcorn as a potential aphrodisiac! Was falling in love always this much fun?

When you're looking for someone very special, what's the fastest way to find him? If you're Pepper, the resourceful and constantly astonishing heroine of **PEPPER'S WAY** (LOVESWEPT #62), you place an innocently provocative ad in your local newspaper that's sure to compel the perfect candidate to respond! Kay Hooper has done it again with this beguiling and whimsical tale of loving pursuit. Thor Spicer answers the ad and suddenly finds himself the object of Pepper's tireless fascination. He's never met a dynamo like this lady before, and his goose is definitely cooked! **PEPPER'S WAY** is a delightfully romantic story, brimming with the unpredictable twists and turns you've come to relish in each new book by Kay Hooper. Perhaps I shouldn't reveal this, but I've always fantasized about having certain of the unusual talents that Pepper reveals to Thor and his friend Cody in this absolutely wonderful love story!

Whew! September positively sizzles with romance that won't fade at summer's end. It's great to know you'll be there to share it with us as the leaves turn those glorious shades of red and gold!

With warm good wishes,

Sincerely,

Carolyn Nichols

Carolyn Nichols
   Editor
LOVESWEPT
Bantam Books, Inc.
666 Fifth Avenue
New York, NY 10103

WILD SWAN

Celeste De Blasis

Author of THE PROUD BREED

Spanning decades and sweeping from England's West Country in the years of the Napoleonic Wars to the beauty of Maryland's horse country—a golden land shadowed by slavery and soon to be ravaged by war—here is a novel richly spun of authentically detailed history and sumptuous romance, a rewarding woman's story in the grand tradition of A WOMAN OF SUBSTANCE. WILD SWAN is the story of Alexandria Thaine, youngest and unwanted child of a bitter mother and distant father—suddenly summoned home to care for her dead sister's children. Alexandria—for whom the brief joys of childhood are swiftly forgotten . . . and the bright fire of passion nearly extinguished.

Buy WILD SWAN, on sale in hardcover August 15, 1984, wherever Bantam Books are sold, or use the handy coupon below for ordering:

SPECIAL MONEY SAVING OFFER

Now you can have an up-to-date listing of Bantam's hundreds of titles plus take advantage of our unique and exciting bonus book offer. A special offer which gives you the opportunity to purchase a Bantam book for only 50¢. Here's how!

By ordering any five books at the regular price per order, you can also choose any other single book listed (up to a $4.95 value) for just 50¢. Some restrictions do apply, but for further details why not send for Bantam's listing of titles today!

Just send us your name and address plus 50¢ to defray the postage and handling costs.